Emily Harvale lives in East Sus
You can contact her via her w
Instagram or Pinterest.

Author contacts:
www.emilyharvale.com
www.twitter.com/emilyharvale
www.facebook.com/emilyharvalewriter
www.facebook.com/emilyharvale
www.pinterest.com/emilyharvale
www.instagram.com/emilyharvale

***

Scan the code above to see all Emily's books on Amazon

Also by this author:

Highland Fling

Lizzie Marshall's Wedding

The Golf Widows' Club

Sailing Solo

Carole Singer's Christmas

Christmas Wishes – Two short stories

A Slippery Slope

The Perfect Christmas Plan – A novella

Be Mine – A novella

***

The Goldebury Bay series:

Book One – Ninety Days of Summer

Book Two – Ninety Steps to Summerhill

Book Three – Ninety Days to Christmas

***

The Hideaway Down series:

Book One – A Christmas Hideaway

Book Two – Catch A Falling Star

Book Three – Walking on Sunshine

Book Four – Dancing in the Rain

Dancing in the Rain

Emily Harvale

ISBN 978-1-909917-19-4

Published by Crescent Gate Publishing

Print edition published worldwide 2016
E-edition published worldwide 2016

Editor Christina Harkness

Cover design by JR, Luke Brabants and Emily Harvale

This book is dedicated to my great friend, Eileen Mills. We've been friends for many years and met when one of us (not mentioning any names) knocked a bottle of red wine over a meat platter, at our office 'do'. No one seemed to notice but we heard several people mention how tasty the selection of meats were, that evening. We still giggle about it after all these years. Oh – and it's Eileen's birthday on October 21st. Happy birthday, Eileen. Thanks for continuing to make me smile. I hope this dedication is a pleasant surprise.

Acknowledgements

My special thanks go to the following:

Christina Harkness for editing this novel. Christina has the patience of a saint and her input is truly appreciated.

My webmaster and friend, David Cleworth who does so much more for me than website stuff.

Luke Brabants and JR for their work on the gorgeous cover. JR is a genius in graphic design and Luke's a talented artist. Luke's website is: www.lukebrabants.com

My fabulous friends for their support and friendship.

All of my Twitter and Facebook friends, and fans of my Facebook author page. It's great to chat with you. You help to keep me (relatively) sane!

To the members of my new Street Team. I love that you want to help promote my books and spread the word. You're the best!

And finally, you – for buying this book. Thank You. It really means a lot to me. I hope you enjoy it.

Dancing in the Rain

Happiness comes when you least expect it

Chapter One

'Rachel Simpson. Stop behaving like a pathetic loser and get out of this car right now!'

Despite her own command, Rachel hesitated and peered through the windscreen. She willed herself to look away, but she couldn't. From where she sat, the row of four Victorian cottages perched on top of Hideaway Cliff beneath an ominous-looking sky, didn't seem quite as appealing as they had on the website for Gilroy's Happy Holiday Cottages. The website photo was obviously taken on a bright and sunny, summer day when the sky was a cloudless baby-blue; the sea a shimmering turquoise mirror, and the flower-strewn fields, a kaleidoscope of colour.

Now, the drab-looking, rain-soaked fields were an indeterminate greeny-grey, and gun-metal-grey clouds bubbled across the sky like a witch's potion in a giant cauldron that had spilled over into the slate grey sea.

'C'mon Rachel. How bad can it be? You've seen the photos. Ivy Cottage is really pretty on the inside. A cosy cottage with a wood burning stove and comfy-looking sofas. Be grateful for small mercies.'

But she had the unpleasant impression of being cocooned in a shroud of grey, and it was getting darker with every passing minute. In this light, or should that be, lack of light, the cottages looked a bit... creepy. A creepy-grey. She was beginning to wish that she and Sonia, her flatmate and best friend, hadn't spent last night binge-watching horror-cum-slasher movies on Netflix. Her imagination was starting to run riot.

'Get a grip, woman!' She tutted loudly. 'And for Heaven's sake... Stop. Bloody. Talking. To yourself!' She tutted again, realising the irony of that statement. This had to stop. Right this minute.

For the umpteenth time, she silently cursed her well-meaning Auntie Elsie for sending her that pile of self-help and self-improvement books two weeks ago.

'I'm not suggesting you need help, sweetheart,' her aunt had said when she had phoned Rachel to tell her the books were on the way, 'and you certainly don't need improvement. Your uncle and I think you're almost perfect just the way you are, and so do your mum and dad, of course. That goes without saying. Although you could safely lose a few pounds and not look any the worse for doing so. A girl can never be too thin, you know. Or too tall. Not that you'll ever be tall, of course. Oh. What was I saying? Oh yes. The books. They did wonders for our darling Margery's *issues*, so I thought they might be of some use to you. You know, sweetheart, to help you get over being tossed aside in such a humiliating fashion by that dreadful Drew fellow. Not that Margery will ever be tall, either. You both take after the Simpson side of the family on that score. And no book will ever be able to help with that. Such a shame.'

Rachel had been tempted to tell her aunt exactly where she could shove her precious books, and that the only reason cousin Margery had any *issues* in the first place was because Margery's mother, namely Auntie Elsie, had insisted on calling her daughter Margery. Poor

2

Margery Simpson had endured more than her fair share of teasing throughout her formative years, due in no small part to her name being so similar to a certain blue-haired, TV character... not to mention margarine, of course. Children and teenagers can be very cruel. And so can some mothers. Even if they don't mean to be.

But Auntie Elsie wouldn't take that kind of comment well, and the last thing any of the Simpson family needed right now was a family feud. Elsie was married to Rachel's, dad's brother, Eric, so Rachel had simply said: 'Thanks, Auntie Elsie. That's really thoughtful of you. I can't wait to read them.' Then she'd skimmed the books when they arrived – in case Auntie Elsie asked questions, which knowing her, she very probably would.

According to many of the authors, the way to be 'a better you' was to tell yourself repeatedly, how wonderful you were. Or how slim, or clever, or whatever else you wanted to be. Who knew it could be that simple? Yeah right. But anything was worth a try, so Rachel and Sonia, had flicked through the books, taking snippets here and there and putting into practice some of the deep breathing exercises and positive enforcement mantras.

The only difference any of it seemed to have made was that both she and Sonia spent a lot more time talking out loud to themselves. And looking in mirrors. It was becoming a rather worrying habit. Especially as it made them notice things about themselves that they hadn't noticed before. Like Sonia unconsciously leaning to her right whenever she wore high heels, and Rachel hunching her shoulders... constantly. But that was as a result of her profession. Rachel spent seven hours a day, six days a week, standing over clients in her mum's thriving hairdressing salon, often performing small miracles on their hair.

3

Rachel stretched her back and breathed in deeply. Craning her neck, her eyes scanned the ever-darkening horizon and the open expanse of empty, grey sea. Even with the car windows shut tight she could hear the waves crashing against the walls of Hideaway Cliff, and a shiver ran through her. A week of fun-in-the-sun this holiday was clearly *not* going to be.

But then she already knew that. She was merely hoping that the weather forecasters would change their minds yet again, and that at least she would have some sunshine, even if there was zero chance of having any fun.

So far though, during the hour and a half journey from an equally miserable-looking, London – weather-wise – she hadn't seen as much as a glimmer of sunshine. There had been several pockets of fog, curtains of misty drizzle, and sheets of heavy rain. All she needed now was a blanket of snow. And she wouldn't be surprised to see it. The temperature seemed to have plummeted by several degrees the further south she had driven and by the time she finally turned into Hideaway Lane – which was extremely well-hidden – the car heater was on the maximum setting.

She had seen little of the village of Hideaway Down as she drove through it and turned up Hideaway Hill towards her destination, but from what she had, the place appeared to be deserted. The outlook definitely wasn't promising.

If only Drew were here. Or Sonia. Or anyone, for that matter. Anyone at all; so that Rachel would not feel so completely and utterly alone.

Sighing deeply, she reached for the raincoat she had tossed onto the passenger seat when she set out on this *little adventure*, as Sonia had encouraged her to think of it, and caught a glimpse of her reflection in the rear-view mirror. Sadness mingled with apprehension flashed before her.

'You can do this, Rachel.' The blue of her irises took on a steely glint. 'You don't need Andrew bloody Walton in your life. You don't need any man. And you're going to have a good holiday, no matter what. Okay?'

But as she stared into the mirror, her resolve quickly melted away.

'You keep telling yourself that, honey. Who knows, one day you may even believe it.'

She shook her head, shrugged on her canary-yellow raincoat and tugged her shoulder-length russet-brown hair free from beneath the collar. Then, with wavering determination she pushed the car door open and stepped from her mud-splattered Ford Focus.

'Bloody hell!' It. Was. Freezing. A gust of icy wind raced over the cliff and slapped her in the face as if to let her know what she was in for.

Rachel's hand hovered over the door handle. Perhaps she could take just a few minutes more to think things through. It was warm and cosy in the car and she still hadn't made up her mind whether to tell the truth and look like a real saddo, or tell a teeny weeny white lie and give the impression that she was a strong, independent thirty-five-year-old, perfectly capable of going on holiday alone… and having a wonderful time.

Okay, that last part was definitely a step too far. Was it even remotely possible to have a wonderful time on holiday alone? She seriously doubted it, no matter how many times both she and Sonia had tried to pretend it could be. And no matter how often she stared into a mirror and repeated it. But then Rachel had never particularly enjoyed being on her own. Neither had Sonia; which was why they still shared a flat together even though they could each afford to rent a place of their own.

The rest of it was plausible though. She could be strong. If she tried hard enough. She could be independent. Well, she didn't really have much choice, did she? Unfortunately, she *was* thirty-five, so it wouldn't be a total lie. And would it really matter anyway? She didn't know a soul in Hideaway Down. She didn't know anyone in the whole of East Sussex. So what was the harm?

No. A lie is a lie, no matter what colour you try to paint it. She was single now and she had better get used to it. And rejoice in the fact, as those books – and Sonia – had been telling her for the last couple of weeks.

Strictly speaking though, she and Drew were only 'on a break'. At least that was what Drew had said: "We need to take a break, Rach." Those were his very words. He had not *actually* dumped her. He had not said it was over between them. Not in so many words. But his secretary, Jenny, had. She had told Rachel, in no uncertain terms, that Rachel and Drew's three-year relationship was well and truly over. Finished. Caput. Terminated.

Rachel tutted. 'Take a bloody break!' She had completely misunderstood what Drew had meant when he had uttered that well-worn phrase. She thought he had meant they needed to get away for a while; to spend some time together in a secluded and romantic hideaway and rekindle some of the passion that even she had begun to realise they had lost. To take a break as in, "Let's go away somewhere together, Rach", but no, that was not, apparently, what Drew was suggesting.

But as Rachel told Sonia afterwards, it seemed like far more than mere coincidence that she had been browsing holiday cottages online just moments before

Drew had Skyped her that day. So when the fire alarm in the Edinburgh hotel where Drew was staying overnight on business, had suddenly – and deafeningly – interrupted their call, she had seen that as an omen. And when she had taken into account the fact that she had been positively drooling over the photos of the interior of one cottage in particular – and that cottage was called Ivy Cottage, and Ivy was Drew's mum's name... added to which, Ivy Cottage was suddenly re-available due to a cancellation – well, anyone could have made the same mistake. Couldn't they?

Two hours later, when she'd finally managed to get back in touch with Drew, she had been thrilled to tell him that she had booked a week away and they would be celebrating their three-year, dating-anniversary in a cute Victorian cottage outside an even cuter village, nestled between the East Sussex Downs and the English Channel.

But Drew had not been pleased. Rachel could still feel the way her heart had fallen from her chest to her stomach and twisted into knots, as Drew explained what he had meant. Well, not explained, exactly. More like... ranted.

'You've done what, Rach?' His brows had furrowed and his lovable lips had sunken into an almost clown-like frown. She could virtually feel his exasperation seeping through the screen of her laptop. 'Why would you book a remote cottage for us to spend time together when I've just told you that I think we need to spend some time apart? We need a break, Rach. A break from each other. Not a romantic getaway. Sometimes, I really wonder what goes on in that head of yours. I've got to go. That sodding fire alarm really screwed things up. We were standing outside for over twenty bloody minutes and then I had to have a couple of whiskies in the bar, to warm myself up. I've got to finish my notes for my meeting in the morning. We'll talk about this when I get back tomorrow night. I really think it's for the best.'

But after he rang off, they didn't talk about it again. They didn't talk about anything again because no matter how often Rachel tried to speak to him over the course of that week, Andrew Walton was out, or in a meeting, or otherwise engaged and unable to take her call.

Neither was he to be found at home. She had gone round to his flat on at least three occasions and not once had he answered the door. She had left him a note; he hadn't replied. She had sent him texts; he hadn't responded. He had blocked her from his Facebook page – although she'd been sure that was an error... at first. As a last resort she had gone to his office, in spite of the fact that she knew Drew would be cross about it. And that was when she had finally got his message loud and clear. Not from Drew. She got it from his heavily pregnant secretary, Jenny.

Rachel had sneaked past the receptionist who was so busy flirting with a motorbike messenger that an army could have marched across the marble-tiled entrance lobby of Morcross James Financial Solutions, and the giggly nineteen-year-old would not have noticed. Although to be fair, even from the back view, the tall, hunky messenger did look hot in his black leathers. After a quick glance, Rachel had jumped in the lift and got off at the third floor, turned right towards Drew's office and bumped slap-bang into Jenny. Or more specifically, Jenny's rotund belly.

The rosy glow had drained from Jenny's exceptionally beautiful face and she looked at Rachel as if she carried the Zika virus, or something equally threatening to pregnant women. But Rachel had always known that Jenny didn't like her. The feeling was mutual.

'Rachel!' Jenny's green eyes flashed as she fired words at Rachel like an automatic weapon. 'You shouldn't be here. Please don't make a scene. Drew hates scenes. Especially at the office. Hasn't he made it clear that it's over between you two? This is really upsetting him, you know. Your constant calls and texts aren't going to get him to come back to you. Isn't it time you stopped harassing him? You're only humiliating yourself. I'm saying this for your own good, Rachel. Please leave us alone. I mean… leave Drew alone. Please go. You know you shouldn't be up here. I see you haven't even got a pass. Don't make me call security.'

Rachel had stared dumbfounded at Jenny's tummy. She half expected an alien to burst out of it and bite her head off, literally. It felt as if Jenny had already ripped out her heart.

So that was it. Drew didn't want to 'take a break'. As far as he was concerned, he had ended his relationship with Rachel. He simply wasn't man enough to say the actual words. And from the size of Jenny's belly and the 'us' Jenny had inadvertently let slip, Drew had begun another relationship at least eight months earlier. Although that surprised Rachel more than anything else. Drew had always said that the one thing he hated, the one thing he would never, ever do, was to cheat on someone he was in a relationship with. His father had cheated on his mother and he still found the fallout from that difficult to deal with, ten years later. So, how or why he had been able to continue seeing Rachel and date Jenny at the same time, she did not understand. Especially once he knew about the baby. But then, Drew wasn't good at making choices. He couldn't even decide what to have when they went out to eat without going over and over what was on offer on the menu, and why one particular

9

dish might be preferable to another. It was the same with wine. Or clothes. Or anything requiring a choice. Drew took forever to decide. It was one of his lovable little quirks.

'Lovable little quirks, my arse!' She had to stop going over this. It was over and she was going to have to spend the week in Ivy Cottage on her own. 'And while you're at it,' she said, giving herself a scolding glare in the faint reflection in the window of the car door. 'Stop bloody talking to yourself! Because we all know where that leads, in spite of what any of those damn books may have told you.'

Rachel slammed the door shut and stepped away from the vehicle. She wouldn't spend another fifteen minutes cosseted within its relative safety. Rachel Simpson had to face the world. And face it with her head held high.

Not that there seemed to be much 'world' to face. The row of four quaint-cum-creepy cottages were in darkness apart from the one closest to where she stood. There was a glimmer of light in one of the two ground floor front windows, and behind the drawn curtains, a silhouette of a man and woman embracing. Well, it looked as if they were embracing. Of course he could be… strangling her…

A ripple of ice slid down Rachel's back, but that was mainly due to the bitingly cold, October evening air and only in part, to her over-active imagination. She dashed to the boot, retrieved her luggage and marched across the muddy gravel parking area and up the brick-paved path to the door of Holly Cottage. She had been sent instructions to collect the key to Ivy Cottage from there. The wind whipped up a pile of damp autumn leaves and a kaleidoscope of greens, purples and reds danced around her. Were they spurring her on or mocking her? She

10

wasn't quite certain which. The earthy scent wafted towards her nostrils; the leaves floated to the ground until another gust swept them upwards. Some were too wet and they lay on the path in a patchwork blanket of colour.

It was incredibly cold and goosebumps prickled her arms as another shiver ran up her spine. She rang the doorbell of Holly Cottage and waited, hoping this was just a cold snap and not an indication of the weather for the week ahead.

Before she booked this break, a mere three weeks ago, the forecasters had predicted an Indian summer for the entire month of October and warmer than usual weather for November. She should have known better than to believe the long range weather forecast. Two weeks ago (one week after that Skype call with Drew) they had changed their minds. They predicted: "unusually warm but with a possibility of some cold snaps together with intermittent, heavy rain showers and strong winds". Three days ago that had changed again, to: "possibly the windiest and wettest last week of October for several years". Talk about from one extreme to another. She wouldn't be surprised if there was a hurricane – like that one way back in 1987 that her mum still talked about and which, apparently, most of the weather-bods hadn't even seen coming. They were so sure it wouldn't reach British shores. Perhaps Rachel should have taken Sonia's advice and stayed at home after all.

'Stay here,' Sonia had suggested as Rachel was preparing to leave. 'The weather's turned really crappy and you hate being on your own. If the weather had been good, there'd be a chance of you meeting people out and about, but if it's going to be anything like they are now saying it is, you'll all be battening down the hatches and

11

staying indoors. You'll hate it.'

'Probably,' Rachel agreed. 'But I really think I need to do this. I've never been away on my own, and I'm thirty-five. It's about time I tried it. Besides, Mum rearranged all the staff rotas at the salon so that I could have this week off. I can't mess them all about. And Mum said that she's really proud of me for doing this. So I definitely can't wimp out of it. Plus... I need a change of scene. Somewhere that doesn't remind me of Drew and me, everywhere I look.'

Sonia jumped in: 'Yeah, so go to Barbados or somewhere exotic and fun. Not some old cottage in the middle of nowhere. I wish I could've come with you, but we're short-staffed at the hospital and unless you've booked months in advance – or a relative is knocking on death's door – you've got more chance of winning the lottery than you have of getting time off at that place at the moment.'

'I'll be fine, Sonia. I've packed my iPad and downloaded about a zillion books. I've got my walking boots and my camera. I've got a raincoat and two waterproof jackets. I'm prepared. And if the worst happens and I hate it, I've got my trusty car to bring me home.'

'If it's not swept away in a deluge.'

'That's my Sonia. Always looking on the bright side of life.'

Although from where Rachel stood now, Sonia may have been right. Those clouds were growing darker by the minute. A distant rumble of thunder settled the issue.

The door of the cottage opened and a beam of light met Rachel, like a beacon of hope. A woman, around Rachel's own age, with flowing auburn hair, smiled at her.

'Hello. You must be Rachel. I'm Holly. Holly Gilroy.

It's lovely to meet you. Come in, come in. It's getting nasty out there.' Holly held the door open for Rachel to pass.

'Hi, Holly. Yes, I'm Rachel. It's lovely to meet you too.' She stepped inside. 'Thanks. I think it's about to chuck it down again.'

'I think you're right. The weather forecast is particularly cheery, I must say. They predict very strong winds and torrential rain but they haven't given it a name yet so it's not officially a storm. I don't know why they do that – name storms. It doesn't make them sound friendlier or anything. Anyway, don't worry. I'm sure you and your boyfriend will find plenty to keep you occupied, no matter what the weather throws at us all. Has he gone straight to the cottage?' She turned her head. 'Gabriel! Will you throw me the key to Ivy Cottage, darling?'

Rachel gulped. 'Um. About that. My boyfriend isn't here. That is… he isn't coming. I mean. Um. He's not my boyfriend. We're not together anymore.'

'Oh, I'm sorry. Are you here on your own?'

Rachel nodded. Holly seemed nice, but she was clearly surprised. She probably thought Rachel was a complete saddo.

'My best friend, Sonia, who's a midwife, couldn't get time off or she would've come with me, but it's fine. I've never been away on my own before, but I needed a holiday. I'm a hairdresser and it's been really hectic at the salon. It's my mum's, and she juggled the rotas when I told her I wanted to book this. Then things changed, of course, but I decided this would do me good. I'm looking forward to the peace and quiet. And I've got lots of books to read and…' Great. She was rambling like a lunatic and the gorgeous hunk who was heading towards them, dangling a key in his hand, was giving her a distinctly odd look.

'Hi, Rachel,' the hunk said. 'I'm Gabriel, Holly's boyfriend. This is the perfect place if you want to be alone. But if you don't, it's also the perfect place to meet people. We're all extremely friendly in Hideaway Down. A word of warning though. Some of the locals think it's their God-given right to poke their noses into other people's lives. Don't take it personally. Just tell them politely, to mind their own business.'

Holly laughed. 'You're joking, aren't you? Since when did being polite to the busybodies of the village ever stop any of them?'

Gabriel smiled lovingly and wrapped an arm around Holly. He shrugged and grinned at Rachel.

'Holly's right. Sorry, Rachel. You'll have to ignore them. The good news is, most of the locals are genuinely lovely. Here's the key. Do you need a hand with your luggage?'

'No thanks, I'm fine.' A village full of nosey people – oh joy. That was just what she *didn't* need right now. At least Gabriel was honest and straight to the point.

Holly smiled. 'There's a welcome pack in the cottage, along with some provisions. Just milk and bread and stuff but if you need anything, don't hesitate to come and ask.'

'Yes,' Gabriel added. 'And in case you haven't come across one – the Range in the kitchen isn't just a cooker, it also runs the central heating. The welcome pack explains it but I made sure there's plenty of wood to keep it going until tomorrow, so you don't have to worry about anything this evening. There's nothing worse than waking up to a stone cold room. Believe me, I know.'

He winked at Holly and she nudged him in the ribs. It was obviously a private joke or something between them.

'Thanks,' Rachel said, 'but my gran has a Range, so I

14

know how temperamental they can be sometimes.'

'Ivy Cottage is right next door,' Holly said. 'We'll let you get settled in but please give us a shout if there's anything you need. We do mean that. I can cook breakfast for you if you like, and make afternoon tea, but some people prefer to do their own thing. Put the empty milk bottle outside the door at night with a note in it saying how many bottles you want each day. Our milk comes from Hideaway Farm and it's delivered by Harry. Harry Goode. He's the son of the owners, Beth and Henry and they all run the place together.'

A crash of thunder boomed a short distance away.

'I think you'd better get to Ivy Cottage,' Gabriel said, half smiling, half frowning. 'We can give you the who's who in Hideaway Down another time. But if you fancy a trip to the local pub this evening, we'll be leaving here at eight-thirty. You're welcome to join us.'

'Thank you. That's really kind, but it's been a pretty hectic week and I think I might just have a quiet evening in and an early night. Another time, perhaps?'

'Anytime,' Holly said. 'My mum owns the pub as well as these cottages, so we're in there quite a bit.'

Gabriel grinned. 'Most of the village is in there. It's called The Snowdrop Inn, but it's the only pub in Hideaway Down, so you can't miss it.'

Another thunderous roar, this time directly overhead.

'Did you feel that?' Holly gasped. 'I swear that one shook the cottage.'

'I'd better dash,' Rachel said, turning towards the open door. 'Thanks for everything. See you tomorrow maybe.'

She raced down the path from Holly Cottage and could only just hear Holly and Gabriel's 'goodbye for now' as the heavens opened. By the time she tumbled into the hall of Ivy Cottage, she was soaked to the skin.

Not a great start to the week – and yet... she had just met two of the nicest people she could possibly meet. This week might not be as bad as she had dreaded it might.

Apart from the weather, of course.

Chapter Two

Lucas Webb peered into almost complete darkness through the torrent of water pouring down his windscreen. He wiped the inside of the glass with the sleeve of his Gore-Tex jacket but it made little difference. He knew there were four cottages out there somewhere but he could only see lights from two of them, fifty feet or so ahead.

'What an *excellent* idea this was, Monty.' He flicked on the interior light and glanced in the rear-view mirror, towards the back seat of his Vauxhall Insignia.

Monty nodded his head in obvious agreement, and barked once. He stood up, stretched his paws out in front of him, yawned, and nuzzled Lucas' shoulder before turning in a circle and collapsing back down onto the tartan blanket spread across the rear seat.

Lucas twisted round and petted his dog. 'We can't sit here all night, boy. I'm not eager to get drenched either but we're going to have to make a run for it sooner or later.'

Monty raised a furry brow, licked his lips and hid his face under his paw.

'I reckon it'll take us five minutes to run to Holly Cottage, get the key and then dash to the one we're staying in.' Lucas pulled his phone from his jacket pocket and swiped the screen. 'Mistletoe Cottage. That's what the place is called. Sounds warm and welcoming, don't you think? Let's hope it's one of the two which have lights on. So… You with me?'

Monty emitted a low growl from deep within his throat, glanced up at Lucas and quickly looked away.

'I guess that's your way of saying: "No way, loser. You got us into this. You get the key… and an umbrella. I'll wait here." Am I right?'

Lucas couldn't be absolutely sure. Dog language was as foreign to him as was Chinese, but in the seven years he and Monty had been together, Lucas believed he was usually pretty close to understanding what was on Monty's mind. And Monty could read Lucas' mind; Lucas *was* certain of that. Since rescuing the now huge, furry crossbreed, as a puppy, from the edge of a river where some shitty human had left the tiny bundle in a black bin liner, Lucas and his beloved dog had become virtually inseparable. Lucas even took Monty to the office with him, but as Lucas was a partner in the small firm of architects he ran with two of his mates from Uni, Monty was allowed. They all referred to Monty as their 'sleeping partner' – and Monty took his title very seriously. He performed his duties with gusto, only stirring for walks, lunch, and one or two meetings where he knew the clients would be bringing doggy treats.

'Okay then. I'll be a hero,' Lucas said, zipping up his dark-blue jacket and pulling the hood over his blond, shaggy hair – which he'd meant to have cut before he came on this holiday, but he had run out of time. 'You're going to have to go out in this rain sometime this evening. Unless your bladder's a lot stronger than mine. Or the storm subsides.'

Monty grumbled and Lucas opened the driver's door

to get out, but a crack of thunder made Monty sit up and bark. The dog leapt over the seat and was by Lucas's side in a split second. Lucas slammed the door shut and switched on the torch icon on his phone. He grabbed a large rucksack and a holdall, from the boot, and threw them on his shoulder. He shoved a bagful of Monty's toys, food and bedding under one arm, using his elbow to close the boot, which was a bit of a struggle against the wind. Then he made a run for Holly Cottage, Monty literally dogging his footsteps all the way to the front door.

'Wuss,' Lucas said, ringing the bell before rubbing Monty's head. Monty edged closer, attempting to hide between Lucas' legs and Lucas smiled down at him. 'You're safe, boy. I won't let anything hurt you.'

Seconds later, a tall, dark-haired man opened the door, smiled and held a key out to Lucas.

'Hi. I'm Gabriel. You must be Lucas.' He stood aside and held the door open. 'Come in before you get soaked through. Unless you'd rather go straight to your cottage.'

'Good to meet you, Gabriel. Yeah, I'm Lucas and this is Monty.' Lucas took the proffered key. 'Thanks for this. I'd rather get to our cottage, if you don't mind. Monty doesn't like storms and this is building up to be a biggie.'

Gabriel nodded. 'I don't mind at all. There's a welcome pack in the kitchen and basic supplies. Any questions, pop round or, in this weather, call the number I've written on the tag. It's Holly's mobile.'

'Great. Catch you later.' Lucas turned and headed down the path, illuminated by his torch.

'Mistletoe Cottage is the third one along from here,' Gabriel called out. 'We're going to the village pub at eight-thirty. Send Holly a text if you want to join us and we'll wait for you. You can bring Monty.'

'Cheers.' Lucas waved his phone in the air without looking back as he and Monty braved the worsening onslaught, to reach the door of Mistletoe Cottage.

Once inside, Lucas turned on the lights and glanced at his watch. He could murder a pint but it was already eight-fifteen and that didn't leave much time if Gabriel and... Holly were going to the pub at eight-thirty. He would like to get settled in and give Monty his supper, first. Plus, he could use some food himself. But hadn't he read on the website when he'd made the booking, that the local pub served food? He could eat there and it wouldn't take long to feed Monty – or for Monty to eat it. Monty could empty his bowl in a matter of seconds.

Lucas dumped his bags, save for the one with the dog food, and headed along the tiny hall, towards the kitchen at the back of the cottage, with Monty close behind him. Thunder roared overhead and Lucas saw a streak of lightning through the kitchen window. That was quickly followed by even heavier rain. Perhaps he should give the pub a miss. A night in front of the wood burner, a photo of which he'd also seen on the website, was probably a much better idea. And they'd had a long drive down from Oxford.

Another drum roll of thunder with its deafening crescendo made the decision for him. Monty scurried under the kitchen table, sank to the tiled floor and covered his head with his paws. There was no way Lucas could take him out in this weather. Luckily, they had stopped less than thirty minutes ago to top up on fuel and for Monty to have a pee. Hopefully, this storm would move on before Monty needed another.

Lucas took off his jacket and threw it over the back of a kitchen chair. He then went back to his bags, retrieved his iPad, and one of the two dog beds he had brought with him, and set about making he and his best friend feel more at home.

He placed the bed in front of the Range, which was belting out some very welcome heat, and put his iPad on the kitchen table. He tapped the music icon and found one of the compilations of his favourite songs. He turned up the volume and sang along to it even though he couldn't sing to save his life. It didn't drown out the noise of the storm but it did make Monty lift his head and join in, barking and howling wherever it seemed appropriate.

'That's my boy,' Lucas said, reaching under the table to pet him. 'Go lie down in your bed, it's more comfortable than the floor and I'll bring your supper over in a sec.'

Monty's ears pricked up at the word 'supper' and with a bark and the scratching, scuttling sound of claws on tiles, Monty darted to his bed, jumped in and sat down, eyeing Lucas over the kitchen table.

Lucas poured food into Monty's bowl and placed it on the floor where Monty hoovered up his meal in the time it took Lucas to fill the kettle and check out the welcome pack which was on the worktop. Beside the folder of instructions and information, which Lucas read whilst waiting for the kettle to boil, there was a box of groceries consisting of a loaf of bread, a packet of digestive biscuits, a small box of teabags and a jar of instant coffee, a jar of what looked like homemade jam and a note saying that there was butter, milk and a piece of cheese in the fridge.

'A gourmet's delight,' Lucas remarked, holding the note in the air for Monty to see, but Monty's head was still buried in his bowl as he licked up every last scrap of his food. 'A night without alcohol won't kill me, I suppose. And bread and cheese isn't so bad.'

Lucas glanced through the window at the darkness

and the torrential rain lashing against the glass. Who was he trying to convince? Himself or his dog. What he really wanted was a pint and a curry. Or anything hot and spicy. No point in thinking about that though. Unless this storm abated pretty smartish they wouldn't be going anywhere. It definitely looked like it was going to be a night in front of the wood burner for him and Monty.

So much for getting away to the seaside and long walks on the beach, followed by fish and chips, or curry and a beer. Bread and cheese, washed down with instant coffee was on his menu tonight. He could stretch to melted cheese on toast. At least that was hot even if it distinctly lacked spice. The cupboards would be empty, of course, although to his surprise when he checked, one did contain salt and pepper pots, both of which were full. That was something.

He made himself a mug of coffee and peeled open the packet of digestive biscuits. He'd have a couple to ward off the hunger pangs that were suddenly poking at his stomach. He pulled out a chair and Monty glanced at him as the wooden legs scraped across the tiled floor. Satisfied that the noise didn't pose a threat, Monty returned his attention to his empty bowl, just to check he hadn't missed a scrap, and Lucas settled back into the chair and watched the lightning extravaganza, for want of anything better to do.

Wait a minute though.

Lucas sat upright and glanced at his watch. Gabriel and Holly would have left for the pub by now but he had a phone and he had Holly's number. Gabriel had said that he could text or call if he needed anything. Well, he needed the number of the nearest Indian restaurant. He could Google it, but personal recommendation was a far better bet. He hoped it wasn't miles away… and that there was a delivery service, no matter what the weather.

He retrieved the key from his jacket pocket, and was about to dial the number written on the tag, when his phone went dead. Damn. He had forgotten to charge it before they'd set out this afternoon. Never mind. He could plug it in and then make the call.

He went to the hall to retrieve the charger from his holdall and returned to the kitchen to plug it in. The storm seemed to be gaining strength; only a few seconds between each clap of thunder now and the kitchen was beginning to resemble a disco as the lightning danced across the sky and lit up the entire room in bright, white light. Monty had returned to his bed but he looked as if he was ready to make a run for the relative shelter of the kitchen table at any moment.

'It's okay, boy,' Lucas said, reassuringly. He flicked on the switch to charge his phone. 'We're safe in here.'

There was a deafening boom of thunder accompanied by several streaks of lightning and as Monty scampered from his bed towards Lucas and the table, all the lights in the cottage went out.

Chapter Three

Rachel screamed involuntarily as all the lights in her cottage went out and she was plunged into darkness.

She had just sat down to eat a plate of steaming hot chilli and boiled, wild rice. Although she tried to calm herself by reasoning that the loss of power was due to the storm – and not the work of some knife-wielding maniac about to murder her – her heart thumped against her chest almost as loudly as the thunder overhead.

'Take deep breaths,' she told herself. 'There's no need to panic. It's simply the storm.'

A large sheet of lightning lit up the kitchen and Rachel spotted her phone on the worktop. She'd left it there after calling Sonia to tell her that she had arrived safely and was settling in. She'd also told Sonia that things might not be too bad because Holly and Gabriel seemed very nice and had been extremely friendly and welcoming, and the cottage was just as warm and cosy as it had looked in the photos on the website... once you got inside and closed the door. That was before the storm had taken hold.

She got to her feet and edged her way around the table. Without lights it was unbelievably dark and she suddenly realised that there were no street lamps up here.

That in itself was pretty unnerving.

A further streak of lightning gave her the few seconds she needed to locate and retrieve her phone. She swiped the screen for the torch icon.

And then there was light... and she breathed a sigh of relief, although she wondered if all this lightning was the reason for the power loss – and hoped it hadn't hit anyone, or anything. She had never seen a storm like this one.

So... what was she supposed to do now? Holly had told her that they were going to the pub, so there was no point in nipping next door to Holly Cottage. She'd heard muffled sounds of music and a barking dog from the cottage on the other side of hers. Perhaps she should go and see if only her cottage was affected or if the entire row was blacked out.

Hadn't she seen some candles in one of the cupboards? She'd thought that was rather romantic and had quickly shut the door on them, but now she realised they may have been there for far more practical reasons. Perhaps this happened a lot. Rather fun if there were two of you; not so much when you were on your own... with only a vivid imagination for company.

She had also seen a mobile phone number on the key tag, with 'Holly' written beside it. She could send Holly a text and ask whether she should do anything, or if she should just sit and wait it out until the power returned.

Assuming it did return. What if it didn't? What if the power lines had been struck? Would the electricity board send people out to fix them in this weather? Could they be fixed, even?

Yes, of course they could. She was letting her imagination get the better of her again.

'You're a strong, independent woman, Rachel Simpson. Get a grip. And get those candles. What's that saying? When life gives you lemons, make lemonade. Well, when life gives you darkness, make your own light. Okay, that saying won't catch on anytime soon, but you get the…Oh, for God's sake, Rachel! Will you stop bloody talking to yourself.'

Silently cursing her aunt for sending her those books, and using her phone torch to see her way, Rachel stomped over to the cupboard where she'd seen the candles. She took six saucers from another cupboard and placed a candle on each, positioning the saucers around the room, so that when lit, the candles would give the best illumination possible.

She lit each candle in turn, adjusting the positioning of one or two, and sat down again to eat her meal.

'This isn't so bad,' she said, tutting as she realised she was talking to herself yet again. She was just wondering if there was a self-help book to stop you from yabbering away like a mad person when something – or someone – tapped loudly on her kitchen window. She jumped so high that her fork flew out of her hand and landed with a resounding clatter in the sink behind her.

She shot a look at the window and gasped as a face peered in. Oh. My. God! This was like a scene from a horror film. Thunder pealed, lightning flashed and rain pounded the glass. Then a dog barked and scratched at the kitchen door, followed by comparative silence apart from the wind rattling the window frames and the rain splattering against the panes… and the sound of Rachel's thumping heart.

A few seconds later a muffled, male voice called out: 'Hello! I'm staying next door. The lights have just gone out. Hello. Can you hear me in there?'

Above the din of the storm, and the barking dog, Rachel realised this person was no mad killer. Well, he could be, but the chances of that were fairly slim. She

26

leapt to her feet and opened the kitchen door, staggering backwards as a wave of rain and wind thudded into her, followed by the muddy paws of an incredibly big, wet dog. All the candles blew out and she was surrounded by darkness once again, save for the streak of lightning visible through the doorway.

'Monty! Down boy,' the man said, charging forward and reaching for the dog's collar. The dog promptly sat on Rachel's foot.

'Ow! Gosh you're heavy.' Rachel bent down and patted what she hoped was the furry beast's head and he licked her face before a gust of wind slammed the door shut and the startled dog leapt into her arms.

'Monty! No.' The man fumbled in the dark, brushing his hand against Rachel's breasts. Both she and the man said: 'Oh!' simultaneously.

A second later, the man gently but firmly pulled the dog away and when he met Rachel's eyes during the next lightning flash via the kitchen window, he looked truly apologetic. Rachel turned, grabbed her phone from the kitchen table and swiped the torch on before the darkness engulfed them once more.

'I'm so sorry about that,' the man was saying. 'Monty doesn't usually jump up at strangers. He's pretty well-behaved, normally. The storm's thrown him off kilter. He hates storms. Sorry. I'm Lucas and this is Monty.'

Lucas, who was rather attractive but somewhat dishevelled, stepped forward, his hand extended towards her. Instinctively, Rachel stepped back.

'You're not going to leap on me and lick me too, are you?' She met a startled look as she shone the beam of the torch directly into his face.

'What? No, of course not.' He held his hand in front of his eyes. 'D'you mind shining that somewhere else, please? You're blinding me.'

27

'Oops.' She lowered the beam. 'Sorry. And I *was* joking.'

'Oh. Thanks.' He blinked a few times. 'Look, I'm sorry to trouble you, but I saw a glimmer of light coming from your cottage. You have candles, I see. You're obviously more prepared for this weather than we are.'

'We?' He was probably here on a romantic break with his girlfriend. Or his wife. Or possibly his boyfriend.

'Me and Monty,' he said, affectionately rubbing the dog's head.

'Oh. Um. No. I wasn't at all prepared for this weather. I was still hoping the sun would come out after the first rumble of thunder. Don't you have candles in your cupboard then?'

He frowned. 'I didn't notice any. Is that where you got yours from?'

'Yes. And if you'll hold my phone, I'll relight them.'

'You hold the phone. I'll light them,' Lucas offered.

Rachel passed him the box of matches from where she'd left them on the worktop. 'Did you have an accident? There's a tear in the sleeve of your jacket.'

'What?' Lucas glanced at his arm and shrugged as he lit the first candle. 'I must've done that when I climbed over the garden fence. I hope you don't mind us barging in on you like this but... oh. You were having your supper. Sorry.' He frowned again as he spotted the single plate and glass on the kitchen table. 'Just one plate? Are you here on your own? Did you tell me your name, by the way? I think I missed it in the... general confusion.'

'I'm Rachel. And yes, I'm here on my own.' She raised her hand to her cheek. Why was she blushing? She needed to make light of this. 'I don't even have a dog.'

Lucas grinned and his blue eyes twinkled in the glow from the candle he'd relit – until Monty shook himself and showered both Lucas and Rachel with water.

'Want one?' Lucas asked, frowning at Monty.

Monty barked, glanced at Rachel then at Lucas and trotted to his master's side.

'I think he has other ideas, but thanks.' Rachel brushed droplets of mud from her jeans and jumper. 'It's a tempting offer.'

'Not only have we ruined your quiet evening but Monty's also splattered you in mud. I'm so, so sorry. I only wanted to see if the power outage had affected all the cottages. And to see if I could borrow a phone. I'm starving and I really don't fancy bread and cheese.'

He finished lighting the candles and turned to face Rachel. Something flickered in his eyes but it was gone in a moment and he looked away.

'Didn't you bring anything with you?' Rachel asked.

Lucas shrugged again. 'Left in a bit of a rush. I brought loads of food for Monty but I meant to stop at Tesco or somewhere to get a few supplies for me. Then the weather turned and I thought it was better to just get here and sort something out later. I figured I'd feed Monty and then perhaps pop down to the local pub for a pint and a bite to eat. Only now...' His voice trailed off as another crack of thunder made Monty whine and try to bury his head between Lucas's legs.

Rachel glanced at her plate of chilli, which was getting colder by the second. 'Look, I've made way too much chilli and wild rice. I seemed to forget I was only cooking for one. Anyway, there's plenty of both left in the saucepans, so if you don't mind spicy food, you're welcome to join me. And I've got plenty of red wine. But no beer, I'm afraid.'

Lucas seemed unsure but Monty looked at the door, glanced up at him and barked.

'I think he's saying that he doesn't want to go out

29

there again just yet,' Rachel added. 'It's up to you though.'

'You clearly speak dog. I think that's definitely what he's saying. But I don't want to be in your way or anything.'

Rachel walked to the cupboard and took out a second glass. 'Yeah. Because it's so obvious that I've got big, exciting plans for this evening, isn't it? This storm was bad enough but now the power's out, I've been imagining all sorts of things. It would actually be quite good to have some company. Grab a plate from that cupboard and help yourself.'

'Well, if you're sure. Thanks. It smells wonderful. And I love spicy food. In fact, the hotter, the better.' Lucas took off his jacket and hung it over the back of one of the wooden chairs. 'What sort of things were you imagining? Being struck by lightning, or the roof caving in, you mean?'

Rachel was pouring him some wine but she stopped in mid-flow. 'Thanks very much. No. Neither of those things had occurred to me – until now, but I'll add them to my list. I was thinking more along the lines of a knife-wielding maniac or something.'

Lucas laughed. 'In this place? It's a bit off the beaten track for that, isn't it?'

'That's precisely where you're likely to find one – the last place you'd expect to.'

'I'll take your word for that.' He grabbed a plate from the cupboard that Rachel had pointed to and, using the ladle she had left in the spoon holder on the worktop, he helped himself to three large spoonfuls of chilli and one of rice. He looked over at Rachel and a wicked smile crept over his face. 'Did you think that was what I was when I knocked on the window?'

'Yep. And I was so startled that my fork flew through

the air and landed in the sink.'

She placed the glass of wine on the table, opened a drawer and took out more cutlery.

Lucas tipped his head to one side. 'What makes you so sure I'm not, then?'

'Well for one thing,' she said, passing him one of the forks, 'you told me you were staying next door, and I decided the chances of a mad killer renting a quaint holiday cottage were fairly slim. And for another, you've got a dog.'

Lucas sat down and smiled at her. 'Don't killers have dogs?'

'I don't think that knife-wielding maniacs would, do you? I can't imagine one of them going on a killing spree, then dashing home to feed his dog and take it out for a walk, somehow.' She tested her food and found that it was still surprisingly warm so she sat down opposite Lucas and was about to tuck in when he raised his glass.

'Cheers,' he said. 'Thank you so much for this. You're a real life saver.'

'Cheers,' she replied, raising her glass. 'You might not say that once you've tried it. I'm not a brilliant cook.'

Lucas took a mouthful and closed his eyes, reopening them a moment later and staring into Rachel's.

'You are so wrong about that... Rachel. You are both a life saver and a brilliant cook. This is the best chilli I think I've ever tasted.'

Rachel blinked several times. Was it the fact that he'd said what he had, or the way that he'd slowly spoken her name that was sending tingles all over her body? Or the way he was looking into her eyes? Or was it merely the storm and the candlelight and the fact that she was really pleased that she wasn't having to spend her first evening completely on her own?

Whatever it was, Rachel didn't care. She was sitting

across the table from a rather handsome man, who looked pretty fit from what she could tell; they were drinking wine and eating a candlelit dinner. Compared to how she expected this evening to turn out, this was nothing short of a miracle. And she even liked his dog. Although the bundle of fur did seem to have a penchant for sitting on her feet. She glanced under the table and saw that Monty had his large furry backside on her slippered feet and his massive, equally furry paws on Lucas' boots. He looked so comfy that she didn't have the heart to move him.

'This must've been what it was like to live in this cottage when it was first built,' Lucas said. 'They probably had to use candles. Or possibly lamps fuelled by whale oil, and later, paraffin. There's no gas up here so even when that began appearing in homes in the late 1800s these people wouldn't have been able to get it, and electricity only started being introduced to households after the First World War. Sorry. That sounded like a history lesson. But isn't it strange to think of people living like this?'

'Yep. No torch icons on phones. No phones even. Are you a teacher then, by any chance?'

'What? Oh no. But both my parents are, and I think it's kind of rubbed off on me. Dad teaches history and Mum teaches art. I'm an architect. But I often sound as if I'm giving a lecture, not having a conversation. Or so my ex-girlfriend frequently told me, anyway.'

'Is that why she's an ex?' Rachel saw a flicker of something akin to anger in Lucas' eyes. 'Sorry. That's none of my business. I'm always speaking without thinking… so my ex-boyfriend was always telling me.' She forced a smile.

Lucas brightened. 'It seems we both have faults. If our ex-partners are to be believed. But to answer your question, that was one of the reasons she gave. She dumped me, you see. The other reasons – and there was an entire list, it seemed – were that I spend too much time at work. I don't have any interest in fashion... or fashion sense. I don't like the right films. I like books and I read far too many. Er. What else? Oh yes. I love my dog more than I loved her. Actually, that one I agree with. Oh, and because the relationship wasn't going anywhere. Whatever that means.' He took a large gulp of wine. 'The stupid thing is, now that I'm telling you this, I realise that we didn't really have anything in common, but I was heartbroken when she dumped me. That's why I'm here.'

'Because you're heartbroken?'

Lucas shook his head. 'No. The heartache went away quite quickly but according to my best mates I've been like a bear with a sore head ever since. I'm in partnership with a couple of mates from Uni and they told me that not only was I becoming a right grouch, socially, I was being a pain in the arse at work, too. And that's a definite no-no. We've got a totally laid-back, friendly vibe at the office and there're only the three of us partners – and Monty, of course.' He smiled at that. 'He's a sleeping partner. Anyway, there's us and then five other admin staff, so when one of our little team is off-colour or something, the rest of us really notice. My mates told me I needed some time out. A change of scene and all that – or they must just beat me over the head with the mock-up of the high-rise office building I was working on. I told them I was far too busy to start planning a holiday, especially as it has to be somewhere I can take Monty. Oh, that reminds me of another thing on the ex's dreaded list. The fact that I never go on holiday unless Monty goes too.' He took another gulp of wine. 'I suppose even I can see why that became a bit of an issue.'

'Didn't she like your dog?'

Lucas shrugged. 'Not enough to spend every holiday with, apparently. Anyway, one of my mate's parents had booked the cottage next door – Mistletoe Cottage – for this week and then one of the grandparents had a fall, so my mate's parents needed to deal with that. My mate suggested I come here instead. So here we are.'

'Gosh, that's weird. Not any of the stuff you said, but the fact that they were going to have to cancel at the last minute. I only booked this cottage three weeks ago, and that was because someone else had cancelled. How strange to think that we're both here because other people couldn't be.'

'That is weird, you're right. But I suppose people have to cancel holidays all the time. That's the trouble with making plans. Sometimes they don't work out as we expect them to.'

'You're telling me.' Rachel hadn't meant to say that out loud. It was those bloody books. She'd become so used to talking to herself that it was second nature to say what she was thinking.

Lucas emptied his wine glass and looked her directly in the eyes. 'Why are you here on your own? Or is that none of my business?'

Rachel fiddled with the stem of her glass. 'Um. I may as well just say it. My boyfriend… sorry, I mean my ex-boyfriend, told me he thought we needed a break. I thought he meant a holiday, so I booked this place. It turned out that wasn't the kind of break he had in mind.'

'Shit! That must have been rough. At least he didn't give you a list of your faults though, so that's something to be thankful for. Did he just come right out and say it?'

'He said it via Skype. He also said that we'd talk about it. But he wouldn't take my calls, so we didn't. His secretary finally told me. And no, he didn't give me a list, but *she* gave me something worse. She's several months pregnant and although neither of them mentioned it to me, it seems the baby is very likely, Drew's.'

'You're kidding! I take it, Drew is... was, your boyfriend?'

Rachel nodded. 'I still can't believe it. We'd been dating for three years. Three years tomorrow, in fact. I had no idea he was sleeping with her behind my back. God knows where he found the time. Or the energy. He was always telling me how busy he was and how tired he was. Now I know why.'

'Christ. That's awful, Rachel. I'm so sorry. You know what though? I think we're both better off without them, don't you?'

Until now, Rachel hadn't been totally convinced that she *was* better off without Drew, in spite of the way he had treated her and despite Jenny and the baby... which may even have been born by now, although she was sure she would have heard about it via the grapevine if it had. And even in spite of everything those stupid books had said about valuing one's self and recognising 'toxic' relationships and unreciprocated feelings, Rachel had been 'pining' for Drew. But since arriving in Hideaway Down, things had definitely started looking up. Perhaps Lucas was right. Perhaps she was better off without Andrew bloody Walton.

Chapter Four

'It looks as if the storm is finally moving on,' Lucas said. He was standing at the kitchen sink, having insisted on doing the washing-up, the dishwasher being out of action due to the electricity failure. He stared through the kitchen window into the darkness. 'The time lapse between each boom of thunder has increased and the strength of the lightning seems to be dissipating as do the wind and rain.'

'Thank heavens for that,' Rachel said, drying each item he placed on the draining board and stacking it away in the appropriate cupboard. 'Perhaps we'll get the electricity back on before too long.'

'At least we have light from the candles and heat from the Range. I can't believe how cold it is for October.'

'Don't get me started on the weather,' Rachel replied. She glanced at Monty who was now curled up in one of two armchairs positioned each side of the Range. 'Monty seems to have settled down.'

Lucas looked round and smiled. 'He's certainly made himself at home. It's almost a shame to have to wake him.'

'Do you have to?' Rachel said, without thinking it

through. 'He can spend the night here if you like. He does look very comfy.'

Lucas met her eyes with a surprised and questioning look and the implication of her words suddenly dawned on her.

'Oh!' she added hastily. 'I didn't mean... that is... I wasn't suggesting... um... I just meant your dog could stay...' She was making it worse. How do you tell someone you've only just met that you weren't asking them to go to bed with you?

Lucas came to her rescue. 'Er. That's really kind but if he wakes up and finds I'm not around, he might get a bit frantic. We haven't spent a night apart since I found him.'

That surprised her. 'Not one night? Did your girlfriend always spend the night at your place then? Or did you take Monty with you to hers? Oh God! I've done it again. I didn't mean to say that out loud. Sorry. That's none of my business. Forget I said that.'

She was rather glad they only had candlelight; her face was probably crimson right now. She could feel the heat in her cheeks as she quickly looked away and she lingered over putting the glass she was holding away in the cupboard, moving several others around as if to make space for it.

'That's okay,' he said, his voice sounding as if it was anything but.

Rachel shot a surreptitious look at him. He was staring out of the window, his hands resting on the edge of the sink as if he was deep in thought. He took a long breath and after a few moments, let it out again.

'I hadn't really thought about it,' he said, his voice little more than a whisper. 'But I suppose, when we did spend the night together, it was usually at mine. When I was at her place... well, let's just say, I always went

37

home to sleep. I think I mentioned that she wasn't a massive fan of Monty's, so I rarely took him to her flat. It was an arrangement that suited us all. At least I thought it did.'

'How long were you two together? If you don't mind me asking?'

Lucas turned to face her. 'Too long, I'm beginning to realise.' He wiped his hands on the tea towel she had left draped over the draining board. 'Right. That's the washing-up done. Thanks so much for having us. I expect you'd like us to leave you in peace now.'

'No!' She'd said that way too fast. 'I mean… not unless you want to go. I'm not tired or anything and I could make some coffee.'

'Coffee would be good. But there's no electricity to boil the kettle.'

'No. But there is a Range and water boils in a saucepan almost as fast as it does in a kettle.'

Lucas smiled. 'Let's have coffee then.'

Rachel got a small saucepan out from the cupboard and filled it with enough water for two cups of coffee. Monty briefly opened his eyes as she put the saucepan on the Range. He yawned, glanced around as if checking that Lucas was still there, smacked his lips together and with a soft sigh, as Rachel patted him on his head, he closed his eyes and went back to sleep.

Rachel grinned and as she turned to get the cups from the cupboard, she noticed that Lucas was looking at her. His head was tilted to one side as if he was mulling something over and his eyes glowed with warmth in the candlelight.

Rachel hesitated for a second as their eyes met. Then, for want of anything better to say, she asked: 'Do you take sugar?'

'No thanks.'

She could feel him watching her as she went to the cupboard and a tingling sensation spread over her body. The storm may have moved on but the air in the kitchen was full of electricity.

'I don't know how people coped in the olden days,' she said, trying to relieve the sexual tension she for one, was feeling.

'You seem to be managing pretty well.' Lucas was leaning against one of the worktops, still looking at her as if he had something other than coffee on his mind. 'When the lights went out, you lit candles. And as dumb as this makes me sound, it wouldn't even have occurred to me to heat water in a saucepan to make coffee. Without you, my evening would have been pretty bleak.'

Rachel didn't want to look at him; he was growing more attractive by the minute and although she was single and could do whatever she wanted with whoever she wanted, she wasn't sure she wanted this. Whatever *this* was. They had only just met and things might look completely different in the morning. Did she really want to jump into bed with this guy on the very first night? She was pretty certain that he would be more than willing. She only had to say the word.

Yes. Yes. Yes! Her body was screaming. *You go for it, girl.*

Her eyes were suddenly scanning the length of his body, from the dried mud on his boots, up the mud-splattered denim of his jeans and over his blue wool jumper and folded arms, to his broad shoulders and his firm jaw-line; then his slightly parted, full lips up to those baby-blue, come-to-bed eyes.

He slowly pushed himself away from the worktop, shoved his blond fringe back from his face and stepped towards her.

Rachel took a deep breath and waited.

The doorbell made her jump.

'Hello!' A woman's voice yelled through the letterbox on the front door. 'It's Holly. Holly Gilroy. Are you okay in there, Rachel?'

With a final glance at Lucas's surprised features, Rachel made her way along a strangely illuminated hall to the front door.

'Hello, Holly,' she said, yanking the door open and shielding her eyes from the lantern Gabriel was holding in the air. 'Yes, we're fine thanks.'

'We?' Gabriel queried. 'Is Lucas, from Mistletoe Cottage with you?'

'Yes.' Rachel hoped her cheeks weren't as florid as they felt. 'He saw I had candles and he climbed... came round. We were just making coffee.'

Holly placed a hand on her chest and breathed a sigh of relief. 'Thank God for that. We thought you might be panicking and wouldn't know what to do. The entire village is in darkness. Gabriel and I left the pub just after the lights went out but a tree had fallen across Hideaway Hill and we had to call Henry to bring his tractor and move it, which took much longer than we all thought it would, but we got here as fast as we could. I would've walked across the fields but Gabriel said I was being silly and that the tree would be shifted long before I could get here on foot.' She threw Gabriel a look of irritation but he grinned in response. 'It wasn't. I could've been here and back in that time. But anyway. Are you sure you're okay?'

Lucas came along the hall, followed by Monty, who had clearly been woken up by all the noise.

'We're fine, thanks,' Lucas said.

He stood so close to Rachel that she could smell the faint scent of sandalwood in his aftershave.

'We've brought some lanterns,' Gabriel said, nodding

40

towards the box he held in his other arm. 'As you can see from the one I'm holding, they give off quite a lot of light. We've got more in the boot, so there are plenty for both of your cottages. But everyone's congregating in the pub, and if I know anything about Hideaway Down, it's very likely that it'll turn into an impromptu party. Would you like to come and join us? The drinks are on the house. Well, they're actually on Jamie. Jamie McDay. He can afford to keep the entire village in alcohol for the night. It'll be fun.'

Holly nodded vigorously. 'It will! Please say you'll come. I hate to think of the two of you stuck up here on your lonesome. You're probably bored to death already. And in case you're wondering, this doesn't happen often.'

Rachel was about to say that they were far from bored, but she thought better of it. Instead she said: 'Really? When the lights went out I remembered seeing candles in the cupboard. I thought perhaps this sort of thing was a regular occurrence.'

Holly shook her head. 'Oh no. The candles are there... well, to be honest, I have no idea why they're there. But they always have been. It's one of the 'supplies' that I always keep topped up. I must ask Mum. I never even think about it. I just check that there are six candles in every cottage. Including ours.' She glanced at Gabriel.

'Don't look at me,' he said. 'I always thought the candles were there for people to use if they wanted to have a romantic dinner or something. It's not the sort of thing you're likely to remember to bring on holiday with you, is it?'

'I suppose not.' Holly smiled at Rachel. 'Anyway, I think this is only the second time since I've lived up here that the power has gone out. So... d'you fancy coming to the party at the pub? As Gabriel says, Jamie McDay is there. You do know who Jamie McDay is, don't you?'

Rachel's eyes widened. 'You mean… *the* Jamie McDay? The actor? The real one?'

Holly grinned and nodded. 'Yep. In the flesh. He's dating our friend, Laurel, who owns The Coffee Hideaway in the village. They're usually in the pub on Friday night. Most of the cast and crew are there tonight. You know, from the new *Keep A Lid On It*, film. They've been shooting a big scene up near Hideaway Hole today, so the majority of them came for a pint at The Snowdrop Inn.'

'Including Beatrix Welsley?' Lucas piped up enthusiastically. 'If she's in the pub you can definitely count me in.'

'Yes,' Gabriel said, grinning. 'Her aunt lives in the village. She's married to the local butcher – the aunt, not Beatrix, of course. Although Beatrix is spoken for, I'm afraid. She's dating our local milkman, Harry Goode. Anything can happen in Hideaway Down, believe me. And it usually does.'

'Who's Beatrix Welsley?' Rachel asked.

Lucas met her eyes. 'Oh. She's the newest member of the *Keep A Lid On It*, cast. I read an article about her. She's… she's pretty stunning.'

'Oh.' Rachel tried not to sound jealous. Why should she be? She'd only just met Lucas. So what if the guy had a crush on a film star. It didn't matter to her. Except, for some reason, it sort of did. But only in a teensy-weensy way. 'I'll come too. I know Jamie's dating your friend, but there's no harm in looking, is there? He's drop-dead gorgeous. I can't believe that so many famous people live in such a small village.'

'Yes,' Holly said, linking her arm through Gabriel's. 'There's a very famous author too.'

'Really?' Lucas said. 'Who's that?'

Gabriel laughed. 'No one you'll ever have heard of. And he's not that famous.'

'I'm a big reader,' Lucas said.

'Of romance?' Gabriel grinned. 'Ever heard of Gabriella Mann?'

'I have!' Rachel shrieked. 'Sorry. I didn't mean to shout. I *love* her books.'

'So did my ex-girlfriend,' Lucas added.

'I thought she had died though. Gabriella Mann, I mean. Not Lucas' ex,' Rachel said, hastily.

There was a sad expression on Gabriel's face as he nodded. 'Unfortunately, she has. She was my grandmother. I co-wrote some of her books and continued to write, under her name, when she became too frail to do so. I now write under my own, Gabriel Hardwick, but you won't have heard of me, I'm sure.'

'I have!' Lucas looked astonished. 'This is incredible. I bought your first book last week and I've got it with me in the cottage. I've almost finished it and I think it's brilliant. I can't wait for the next one. Any chance you'll sign it for me?'

Gabriel brightened. 'Absolutely, Lucas. Bring it round tomorrow or the next day and I'll gladly sign it.'

'Wow!' Rachel said. 'Film stars and famous authors. It really does all happen in Hideaway Down, doesn't it? Next you'll be telling us that the empty cottage on the end is going to be rented by some singing superstar or something.'

Holly and Gabriel exchanged glances.

'Well,' Holly grinned. 'We'll have to wait and see who arrives tomorrow, won't we? Grab your coats and let's get to the pub. Lucas, are you bringing your dog? You said his name is Monty, didn't you? I should warn you that my mum has a dog called Merlot and a cat

43

called Mistletoe. They live in the pub and they're both mad, so be prepared.'

'And that's not the least of it,' Gabriel added, glancing at Holly. 'As we were leaving to come here, Meg Stanbridge was heading towards the pub with the Gaggle Gang.'

'The Gaggle Gang?' Rachel queried, grabbing her coat from the coat rack in the hall as Lucas headed to the kitchen to get his jacket and Monty trotted along behind him.

'I'll explain on the way,' Holly said. 'You're not frightened of geese, are you? One or two of our holidaymakers have been.'

'Um. No,' Rachel replied. 'I'm not really frightened of anything. With the exception of knife-wielding maniacs.'

Gabriel gave her an odd look. 'I don't think we've got any of those around here. But some of the *Keep A Lid On It* cast are still in costume, so I hope you don't mind vampires.'

'Nope.' Rachel laughed. She turned to close the door once Lucas and Monty had exited. 'Vampires are fine.'

If anyone had told her that this was how she would be spending the first night of her holiday, she would never have believed them. Not in a million years. And more to the point, she was beginning to think that it might just be possible to go on holiday on your own – and actually have fun.

Who knew?

Chapter Five

The temperature seemed much warmer now than when Rachel first arrived, and the stillness of the night air was incredible after such a violent storm. Not one leaf lifted up from the ground even though the path and surrounding front gardens were covered in them. They were probably all held down by the sheer weight of water that had pelted down; the earth looked sodden and large puddles of rain sat like tiny lakes on the grass.

'Mind where you're walking,' Gabriel said, holding his lantern in the air.

Rachel turned on her phone torch to light the way for her and Lucas, who was walking by her side, and Monty, who was busy sniffing each and every pile of leaves.

The gravel, parking area looked more like a beach than a car park and most of it was under at least an inch of water. Rachel was glad she was wearing boots although she tried to lift the legs of jeans a fraction, to stop the hems from dragging in the wet. It was difficult with only one hand but Lucas, clearly seeing her predicament, reached out and held her phone. It was a wasted effort; Monty charged through the water, sending ripples and splashes everywhere and it wasn't just the hems of Rachel's jeans that got wet. Or Rachel; Monty splashed water over Holly, Gabriel and Lucas, too.

'Monty, no!' Lucas scolded. Which seemed to make Monty think it was a game and he did it all the more. 'Sorry about him,' Lucas apologised, trying to grab Monty but missing. 'One word from me and he seems to do as he likes. Come here, boy.'

'Don't worry about it,' Gabriel said. 'At least he's having fun.'

'Wow! It really did come down, didn't it?' Rachel said, trying to step out of Monty's path as he headed back towards Lucas. 'And yet now, you'd never know there had been a storm. Everything is so quiet and still.'

'Apart from Monty,' Lucas said, grabbing him firmly by the collar. 'He's his own, personal tornado.'

Rachel and the others laughed.

'Yes. Apart from him,' Rachel agreed.

'Er. I think I'd better take Monty in my car,' Lucas said, as Holly opened the passenger door for Rachel to get in to what looked like a brand new Range Rover – save for the mud splatters on the otherwise pristine blue exterior.

Gabriel opened the tailgate. 'It's not a problem, Lucas. We've got an old picnic rug. Monty can sprawl out on that, back here in the load space. And the rear seats are leather, so if he wants to prop his head on those to be close to you, he can. The water will wipe right off.' He grinned. 'It won't be the first time this boot has had a wet dog in it. The first day we got it, we took Janet – Holly's mum – and her dog, Merlot out in it and Merlot dived into Hideaway Hole. That's a lake. Janet decided to jump in after him, even though Merlot can swim better than Janet.'

'Oi!' Holly said, laughing. 'You dived in, too. And had the nerve to pull me in with you. So don't make it sound as if my mum's the only stupid one here.'

46

'That's true,' Gabriel said. 'But it was an incredibly hot day.'

'Yeah, yeah.' Holly climbed into the driver's seat. 'Any excuse.'

Lucas coaxed Monty into the back and then got in beside Rachel on the rear seat. Gabriel sat next to Holly in the front and kissed her on the cheek.

'Let's go,' he said, and without further ado, Holly sped off towards Hideaway Hill and the village.

'That's the tree,' Holly said, pointing to a huge trunk lying at an angle in a field beside the road, lit up in the beam of the Range Rover's headlights. 'It looks even bigger now. And there's Henry!' She beeped the horn and braked, and an arm appeared from a tractor near the fallen tree.

'And Harry,' Gabriel said, waving to a man with something similar to a miner's torch strapped to his head, and who seemed to be removing a chain from the tree trunk. Gabriel opened the window. 'Want a hand?' he yelled.

'Nope,' Harry shouted. 'All good, Goode here, thanks. How are your guests?'

'Rachel and Lucas are fine. They're in the back. We're going back to the pub. You coming?'

'Yep. Just making sure this thing won't fall back onto the road. We'll see you there.'

Gabriel and Holly waved and Gabriel turned to face Rachel and Lucas as Holly continued down the hill.

'That was Harry Goode,' Gabriel said. 'And his dad, Henry, was driving the tractor. We left them to it so that we could check on you. They're two of the nicest people you're ever likely to meet. Mind you, everyone is nice in this place. That sounds like a corny cliché but it's the truth. That's why I stayed. Well that, and because I fell in love with Holly, of course. I only came here to stay for a week's holiday, like you two. But I never left.'

'Wow!' Rachel said. 'Was it love at first sight?'

Gabriel laughed. 'Er. Not exactly at first sight. The first time I saw Holly, she was wearing reindeer print pyjamas. Her hair was piled on her head and tied up with a Christmas ribbon and...' His voice trailed off and he nudged Holly's arm.

Holly glanced at him and grinned. 'And... I had a huge ring of toothpaste around my mouth, which, being a gentleman, Gabriel had decided not to mention. I had no idea I looked like some mad woman until my sister, Ivy, kindly pointed it out to me after Gabriel had left.'

'And the second time,' Gabriel continued, with a huge smile on his face, 'Holly came to the door with a toothbrush in her hand and promptly flicked a globule of toothpaste over my brand new – and very expensive, I might add – coat. I think that was when I fell in love with her. I've always been fond of a woman who takes her dental hygiene seriously.'

'And you, Holly?' Rachel asked. 'When did you know you had fallen for Gabriel?'

Holly shook her head. 'I honestly don't know when the exact moment was. At the time, I was still in love with my ex. At least I thought I was. Then one day I wasn't, and it dawned on me that I had fallen head over heels in love with Gabriel. But it wasn't all plain sailing. Or perhaps I should say skating, as it was Christmas and everything in Hideaway Down was frozen – literally. Or covered in snow. Well, almost everything. Anyway, Gabriel also had an ex and she caused us both a bit of a headache. I'll tell you the whole story later, if you're interested. But for now, this is Hideaway Down and that's St Katharine's Church on our right. There's a footpath from the cottages which comes out right by the church.'

48

'You'll love our vicar,' Gabriel said. 'His name's Kevin Longbourne but everyone calls him Kev-the-Rev, including himself. He even has a variety of T-shirts, in all colours and styles, with Kev-the-Rev emblazoned across the front. He's a real character and a really great guy. Very interesting to chat with, whether or not you're religious.'

'The village looks completely different in the dark,' Lucas said. 'I'm glad Monty and I arrived before the lights went out. I don't think I would've found the cottages in this pitch black.'

'It's quite amazing how much difference electric light makes,' Gabriel agreed.

'We were discussing that earlier,' Rachel said. 'About how the occupiers of the cottages in days gone by would've had to use candles or oil lamps. It's weird to think of people living like that. No TVs, iPods, laptops or anything. What did people do?'

'They spent most of their time working,' Gabriel said.

Holly nodded. 'And cooking and cleaning. There were no washing machines or dishwashers, or fridge freezers. It doesn't bear thinking about. I'm so glad I wasn't alive then.'

'Most of them had big families too,' Gabriel added.

'So they didn't spend all their time working, cooking and cleaning,' Lucas quipped.

Rachel was grateful for the darkness in the car, although why she was blushing at that remark, she had no idea. Perhaps it was because she was pretty sure that if Holly and Gabriel had turned up about fifteen minutes later, she and Lucas may well have been in the middle of a potentially embarrassing situation.

At the very least, she was certain that he had been about to kiss her, although from the look she had seen in

49

his eyes, even in the candlelight, she thought he had a lot more than that on his mind. But she could have completely misjudged the situation. It wouldn't have been the first time that a man had been thinking one thing and she had thought he meant something entirely different. Take a bloody break, indeed.

'Is that the pub ahead?' Rachel asked, keen to stop herself from dwelling on that subject. A brightly lit building appeared a short distance away, although it looked nothing like a pub from where she sat. It seemed to be hovering in the air a few feet from the ground and it shone out in the darkness like some sort of alien spaceship. She vaguely remembered from the photos on the website that the pub sat on a raised bank at one end of the main road through the village. The bank however, blended into the darkness.

'Yes,' Holly replied. 'That's The Snowdrop Inn.'

Rachel could hear genuine pride and affection in Holly's voice.

'Is that where you grew up?'

Holly nodded. 'Yes. With my twin sister, Ivy, and my grandad – who everyone in the village, including the Gilroy family, all call Gramps. My grandmother died many years ago, and Dad ran off with an old girlfriend when we were young, so it's just been Mum, Ivy, Gramps and me for a very long time. But Ivy and I still see Dad at least once or twice a year, and Gabriel's met him. It's a sore subject with Mum though, even after all these years, so please don't mention him to her. The last person who did ended up in the pond outside the pub.'

It was unbelievable how open Holly and Gabriel were. Rachel couldn't imagine telling a virtual stranger such intimate details of her own life, but Holly seemed to have no qualms about sharing personal information. The way she and Gabriel had met and fallen in love; about

Holly and her ex and Gabriel and his. And now about Holly's dad running off with another woman.

Rachel recalled how long she had sat in her car when she arrived, wondering whether to be honest and admit that Drew had dumped her or whether to lie about it so that she wouldn't appear like some sort of sad, pathetic loser because no matter how much she tried to ignore it, he had. But Holly and Gabriel clearly weren't the type to judge. They were simply decent, kind and friendly people who would happily tell you their life stories and not feel in the least bit odd about doing so.

'Does your sister live in the village?' Lucas was asking.

'She does now. She lived in London for some time but last month she moved in with her boyfriend, Ned. Ned Stelling. He owns the smithy, which is virtually opposite the pub, and they live in his flat above. It's been quite an eventful year for Ivy and her life has changed in ways that neither of us would have believed this time last year. She's even just given up her job in London, which none of us ever thought she'd do. She worked in the music business and absolutely loved it but now that...' Holly's voice trailed off and she glanced at Gabriel.

These people really *did* like sharing details of their lives, but there was something about Ivy that Holly clearly thought she should hold back. Or perhaps Holly just meant that now Ivy and Ned were living together, Ivy no longer wanted to work so far away. Rachel was eager to meet her and find out. But would Ivy be pleased that two guests staying at her mum's rental cottages now knew so much about her?

'Will Ivy and Ned be at the pub tonight?' Rachel asked.

Gabriel shrugged, and smiled at Holly. 'They were there we when came to get you, so I expect they still are.

They're… celebrating.'

'Oh?' Now Rachel was even more curious.

Holly pulled into a small parking area at the rear of the pub. 'This is 'hot-off-the-press' and not everyone knows yet. Actually, that's not true. Who am I kidding? This is Hideaway Down. The entire village knows by now even though Ivy and Ned only knew for sure at the beginning of this week and they haven't announced it publicly. They've only told us – and Ned's mum of course.' Holly stopped the car and twisted around in her seat to face Rachel and Lucas. The look of excitement on her face was matched by the tone of her voice. 'Ivy's expecting! And although people say twins are supposed to skip a generation, and Ivy and I are twins, the scan says otherwise. She and Ned are going to have twins in May next year! We're all so excited.'

Chapter Six

The Snowdrop Inn probably hadn't changed that much since the day it was built, Lucas thought as he scanned the interior of the packed pub. By the look of some of the customers, nor had its clientele. A few of them wouldn't have been out of place if a time machine swept them up and plonked them on one of the stools in front of the long bar several hundred years in the past.

One woman in particular caught his observant eye. Her face was that of a cherub's and her head of grey hair, a mass of dishevelled curls. That, together with a dress that appeared to be made from a hessian sack, meant she could easily be a fifteenth-century healer. She was perched on a stool and was leaning against the bar as if she might fall off. Lucas couldn't help but wonder how she had managed to climb onto it. He could tell she was rather short and as she placed one chubby hand on her chest and took several deep breaths, he could see she clearly wasn't in the best of health.

'Lordy, Lordy me,' she said, as they walked towards the bar. 'You poor young dears. What a start to your holiday this is. I expect you were as frightened as lambs when all the lights went out, you were. And you only arrived today, so you did. No time to get your bearings.

You must be gasping for a drink, you must. Soothe your nerves. Pour me another rum and black please, Janet, there's a dear. Then I must get back to my babies.'

Babies? Lucas thought she was far too old to have *babies*, unless she was referring to her cats or something. She looked a bit like one of those 'crazy cat ladies'.

'You two married?' The woman stared directly at him.

'No, Meg,' Holly said, stepping behind the bar and grabbing a bottle of Chardonnay. 'They're not 'together'. Rachel is staying in Ivy Cottage and Lucas and his dog, Monty, are staying in Mistletoe. Rachel and Lucas, meet Meg Stanbridge. Meg's lived in the village all her life and she looks after the Gaggle Gang. They're the geese I think we mentioned to you.'

Lucas couldn't recall hearing about any geese, but he smiled and nodded.

'Good to meet you, Meg,' he said, as Monty bounded past him and started licking Meg's somewhat mud-encrusted boots. 'Monty! Stop that.'

Meg chuckled and, with some difficulty, reached down to pat Monty's head. 'Lordy, lordy me. You're a handsome young boy, you are. Don't you go chasing my darling geese, though, while you're here, or you'll have me to answer to, you will.' She looked Lucas directly in the eye. 'That goes for you too, young man.'

Rachel sniggered behind him.

'And you, young lady,' Meg said, peering around Lucas to glare at Rachel. 'You young girls are just as bad. Had one here in August. Friend of dear young Beatrix, she was. Lucy, I seem to recall. I heard she chased my babies down the length of Market Street after a few too many drinks, she did.' Meg tutted and shook her head.

'Who told you that, Meg?' Gabriel asked, frowning.

54

Meg sniffed. 'Thought you'd kept it quiet, you did, didn't you? Nothing gets past Meg Stanbridge. Lordy, lordy me, it doesn't. I know everything that happens in Hideaway Down, I do.' She took the glass of rum and black that Janet Gilroy placed on front of her.

Janet grinned. 'That's on the house, Meg.'

Meg beamed at her. 'Thank you, dear. You're an angel, you are. I've always said so, I have.'

Rachel looked offended but she smiled at Meg. 'I assure you I won't be chasing anything, anywhere. Or having too much to drink. I know my limit and I stick to it. Most of the time.'

'As do I,' a female voice piped up from behind Lucas. 'These days.'

Lucas glanced round and saw a woman, so similar to Holly in both colouring and looks that she had to be Ivy, Holly's twin sister, although they were definitely not identical.

Meg coughed and gave Ivy a surprised look. 'Limit? Lordy, lordy me, Ivy dear, you shouldn't be drinking at all, you shouldn't. Not in your condition. I believe congratulations are in order, so they are.'

Ivy laughed. 'So you've heard, have you, Meg? I suppose Audrey told you.'

Meg sniffed again. 'Can't divulge where I heard it, just that I did. I think that calls for another rum and black, I do. To toast the baby's well-being.'

She emptied the glass she had just been given and edged it back towards Janet, who shook her head but smiled.

'Of course it does,' Janet said, taking the glass. 'And if I were you, Ivy darling, I'd make a public announcement the minute Ned gets back from the loo. Before someone else does.' She tipped her head slightly towards Meg, who was busy petting Monty again and clearly didn't notice.

Holly agreed: 'Mum's right, Ivy. You know what this place is like. Better that they all hear it from you and Ned.'

'Hear what, Hollyberry? That Ivy here is going to be a mum?' A large, middle-aged man with bushy ginger hair came up behind Holly and gave her a hug, winking at Ivy as he did so. 'I think most of the village knows that by now. Congratulations to you and Ned, Ivy.'

Holly tutted but Ivy laughed. 'Really, Henry? That's great. Saves me having to give a little speech then.' She stared at the bottle of wine Holly was holding. 'Are you going to open that or just cuddle it? God, I wish I could have a glass, but you see, Meg,' she added, nudging Meg's arm, 'I'm being a good girl.'

'Quite right too,' Henry said. 'Beth's already started knitting, you know. So has Petunia, I believe. And Audrey, naturally.'

'Oh joy.' Ivy rolled her eyes. 'I think Audrey got the knitting needles out when Ned and I were still telling her the news.'

Gabriel smiled. 'At least you'll have plenty of blankets and little hats and booties, shawls and cardigans.' He glanced from Ivy to Holly to Rachel, Lucas, Meg, Henry and Janet. 'What? Why are you all looking at me like that?'

Henry slapped him on the back. 'I think we're all surprised you know so much about knitting, lad.'

'I don't. Not really.'

Ivy laughed again. 'That's what comes from writing all those romance novels, Gabriel.'

Gabriel frowned. 'I don't think there was even one baby in any of those books. Not one.'

'Why not?' Meg piped up. 'Lordy, lordy me. Don't tell us you don't like babies as well as not liking dogs.'

'What? Who said I don't like dogs? Or babies?'

'You did,' Ivy said, pointing a finger at Gabriel. 'When you first arrived here last Christmas. There was a dog staying next door and kids in... I forget which cottage but one of them. Or perhaps the kids were next door and... Anyway, you said you didn't like them. Although you did end up playing with the dog and building a snowman with the kids, I seem to remember.'

'That's true, darling,' Holly said. 'I think it was in this very spot too, that you said it.'

Janet nodded. 'Yep. I remember that.'

Henry roared with laughter. 'Me too, lad. You provided the village with plenty to talk about, and I remember you saying you weren't a lover of dogs or children.'

Gabriel let out a sigh of irritation but he smiled. 'I was referring to my new step brothers and sisters, I believe, and I didn't say I didn't *like* them, merely that I didn't want to spend Christmas with them. As for dogs, the only ones I said I didn't like were the ones who bark constantly.'

'That's not the dogs' fault,' Lucas said. 'That's because the owner hasn't trained the dog properly.'

Monty suddenly began barking, loudly and Ivy grinned at Lucas.

'You were saying?'

'Yeah.' Lucas grinned back. 'But Monty likes to show who's boss in our relationship, sometimes.'

'I think that may be more to do with the fact that he's spotted Mistletoe,' Janet said, nodding towards a tortoiseshell cat sitting at the end of the bar.

Another loud bark came from the direction of a room behind the bar and a Red Setter burst out through the open door, followed by an elderly man, carrying a garden gnome in one hand.

'Look what I found in that box I bought at the auction last week,' the man said, waving the gnome in the air. 'Oh. Where's Sarah vanished to? She was here talking to Meg just five minutes ago. I told her I was going to get her something. Where did she go?'

'And now you've met the entire Gilroy family,' Gabriel said, giving Lucas and Rachel a knowing look. 'This is Gramps and the dog is Merlot.'

'She told me she was going to 'powder her nose' but she's talking to Ned,' Ivy said, pointing over her shoulder. 'She accosted him as he came out of the loo. Go and rescue him, Gramps. She's probably giving him a lecture about the fact that we're not married but we're having babies. I'm sure you told her the good news, didn't you?'

Gramps nodded and kissed Ivy on the cheek. 'Of course I did, sweetheart. Can't keep news like that to myself. Besides, Sarah's almost family.' He winked and headed towards the people Ivy had pointed at: an elderly woman, probably of a similar age to Gramps and a man about Lucas' age, who was obviously Ivy's partner, Ned.

'Did Gramps just say what I think he did?' Ivy looked from Janet to Holly. 'Is the old goat actually going to ask Sarah Saltcote to marry him? Because he'd have to. There's no way that woman would consent to living in sin, as she considers Ned and I are doing.'

'I hope so,' Janet said, beaming. 'He can move in with her and I can rent out his room.'

Holly laughed. 'You're still waiting for the builders to carry out the renovations to the other rooms, Mum, and that's being ongoing since last Christmas! Don't be in too much of a hurry to add another room to the list.'

'Bloody builders. Don't get me started on that subject.'

'God no,' Gabriel said. 'We don't want Rachel and

Lucas to think they're renting cottages from a mad woman.'

'I hope they have a church wedding,' Holly said. 'I'd love to be a bridesmaid again and Sarah doesn't have any family, does she?'

'You can be a bridesmaid at my wedding,' Ivy said. She blushed as all eyes turned to her, adding: 'I mean... if and when Ned and I decide to get married, that is.'

'I've never been a bridesmaid,' Rachel said, in a pitiful voice.

'Always a bridesmaid, never a bride,' Meg chipped in. 'If you've never been a bridesmaid, dearie, there's more chance of you getting married, there is. Why, a pretty girl like you should have men eating out of her hands, she should. Why are you here on your own?'

To Lucas' utmost surprise, Rachel suddenly burst into tears, which was weird because she didn't seem the sort of girl to do that. Not at all.

Chapter Seven

Without a word, Holly and Ivy both linked an arm through Rachel's and led her through the door behind the bar into a snug little room with a roaring fire in the hearth and two comfy-looking but well-worn leather wing chairs.

'Sit,' Ivy said, almost pushing Rachel into one of the chairs. 'I'll go and get you a glass of brandy and you can tell us what's wrong.'

'I've got the brandy.' Janet appeared, carrying a large brandy glass which was nearly full to the brim.

'Rachel may not want to tell us why she's upset, Ivy,' Holly said, frowning at her sister. 'You can't just demand to know people's personal stuff. Although she did say when she arrived this evening that she and her boyfriend had split up.' Holly handed Rachel a box of tissues. 'Is that what's upset you, Rachel? Did Meg and the whole marriage thing stir up unwelcome thoughts? I know how awful it is when you're trying to get over someone and people start talking about happy couples or brides or stuff.'

'Drink this,' Janet said, squeezing past her daughters to give Rachel the brandy. 'It'll make you feel better.'

Rachel wiped away her tears and blew her nose. She

eyed the brandy doubtfully. 'If I drink that, I think there's a very good chance it'll make me feel sick. Sorry, but I've never liked brandy. Thank you for the thought though. And I'm sorry about this. I don't have the faintest clue why I suddenly started blubbing like an idiot. I was fine. I *am* fine. Really I am.'

'Oh well, no point in letting it go to waste,' Janet said, knocking back the brandy in just a few speedy gulps while the others watched her. When the glass was empty, she smiled. 'What would you like, sweetie? I'll get you a glass of that instead. Assuming we have it.'

Rachel shrugged. 'Just red wine – but I'm fine, honestly. You don't need to get me anything.'

'You're in my pub and you're upset. You'll have a glass of wine and it's on the house. Don't move.' Janet hurried back into the bar.

'Do you want to talk about it?' Ivy asked. 'Or would you rather we all simply left you in peace? You can stay in here until you feel up to facing everyone again, because I'm sorry to say this but there will be questions… from Meg at least, and probably one or two of the others.'

'Oh no.' Rachel sighed. What did she expect? You can't burst into tears one minute and then act as if you didn't, the next. Of course people would ask why.

Holly nodded. 'Lucas looked very surprised.'

'Lucas? Oh.'

'And he's just asked me if you're okay.' Janet reappeared with a wine glass and a bottle of red. She handed the glass to Rachel and began pouring the wine. 'I thought I'd bring the bottle to save time. Say when.'

'When,' Rachel said, as the glass was rapidly filling up, but Janet kept pouring anyway. 'Stop!'

Janet winked. 'Sorry, sweetie. I didn't hear you. Must be my age. 'I think he's rather taken with you.'

'Who? Lucas? No. We only met this evening.'

'And your point is…?'

'We don't know each other.'

'Haven't you heard of love at first sight?'

'Of course. But…' Rachel took a couple of gulps of wine. She *had* thought Lucas was pretty hot. And she's seen the look on his face just moments before Holly and Gabriel came back to check on them. She was sure he was going to kiss her, so maybe he was attracted to her. It wasn't love at first sight but he could fancy her… couldn't he? 'No,' she continued, after another large mouthful. The wine was going down rather nicely. 'That's ridiculous. Things like that don't happen in real life, only in books and movies. Well, they've never happened to me or anyone I know, in any event.'

'But they do happen,' Janet insisted, pouring some wine into the brandy glass she'd emptied earlier. 'Look at Holly and Gabriel.'

'He seems like a nice guy,' Ivy said, before Rachel could respond. 'And he's not bad looking, either. Want me to do some matchmaking? I'm good at stuff like that.'

'No, you're not,' Holly said, laughing. 'You think you are, but you're not. I remember when I came to stay with you in London for the weekend, not long after Paul and Naomi ran off together, and you tried to fix me up with someone you worked with. We were complete opposites. In every sense.'

'Did I? I don't remember that. What was his name?'

'Nigel.'

'Oh yeah! He was drop-dead gorgeous. Your problem is you've got no taste in men. Well, you didn't have, until Gabriel came along.'

'And your problem was, you put more value on a guy's looks than his personality – until you fell head over heels for Ned, that is.'

'Thanks. Are you saying Ned's ugly but he's got a good personality?' Ivy glowered at Holly. 'Because I'll go and burn down your book shop if you criticise the love of my life.'

Rachel was worried – until both Ivy and Holly burst out laughing and Janet gave Ivy a playful slap.

'You know that everyone thinks Ned's gorgeous,' Janet said. 'Especially you, Ivy. And I think I can safely say that both of my darling girls have changed since last Christmas. For the better, of course. Not that there was anything wrong with either of you in the first place, as far as I'm concerned. But we're supposed to be taking care of Rachel.' She topped up Rachel's almost empty glass

Rachel smiled. 'I'm fine, honestly.' How many times had she said that now? The strange thing was, she was fine. She'd been dreading this week and yet on the very first night she was feeling as if she had already made several new friends. Even if the weather was the worst since records began, she might actually have some fun, after all. So why had she cried? Perhaps it was merely the mention of marriage that had triggered something deep inside and brought it all to the fore. Or perhaps she was simply tired. She hadn't been thinking about Drew. At least, not consciously. 'The plain fact is, Drew was having an affair with his secretary, behind my back and they're going to have a baby.'

Three pairs of startled eyes turned to her, and Holly's mouth even dropped open. Rachel blinked. Oh dear God, had she actually said that out loud? Those bloody self-help books! Auntie Elsie Simpson had a lot to answer for. And not just for being stupid enough to call her own daughter, Margery.

'I think we're going to need another bottle,' Janet

said, squeezing Rachel's shoulder before heading out to the bar.

'Bring a glass for me, Mum,' Holly called after her.

'And me,' Ivy added. 'Oh bugger. I can't drink alcohol, can I? Grab me a coke or something, please.'

'Will do,' Janet yelled back.

'This pregnancy lark is going to be a bundle of fun,' Ivy said, rubbing her tummy even though she was hardly showing. 'I am *so* looking forward to morning sickness and all the others joys Mother Nature has in store for me. And all without the comfort of alcohol.' She let out a massive sigh.

'Ivy!' Holly hissed, nodding her head in Rachel's direction.

'Oh yeah. Sorry, Rachel. I suppose that was pretty tactless, even for me.'

Rachel forced a smile. 'It's okay, Ivy. I don't know why I said that – about Drew and Jenny. That's her name. His secretary. I'm not upset about it. Really I'm not. I hope they'll all be very happy. I just wish he'd had the decency to tell me he didn't love me anymore, that's all. Oh God!'

She burst into tears once again.

Chapter Eight

'But I made a complete fool of myself, Sonia,' Rachel said, putting her phone on loud speaker and placing it on the bedside table. She'd been holding it up to her ear for the last ten minutes and she was getting serious arm-ache. She really must go to the gym when she got home. She couldn't even lift a phone without it hurting. Fitness should be a number one priority, especially as she wasn't getting any younger – as dear Auntie Elsie had a tendency to constantly remind her.

'I'm sure it wasn't as bad as you say,' Sonia tried to reassure her.

'Oh it was, believe me. You should've seen me. One minute we're all chatting in the bar and I'm getting to know the locals – some of whom are really out there, let me tell you. The next, I'm blubbing like a broken tap. Well, not quite that bad, but it just came from nowhere. I think I was as surprised as everyone else.'

'Holly, Ivy and Janet were brilliant from what you said earlier and it was great that, when you did finally go back into the bar, no one mentioned it and just carried on as if nothing had happened.'

Rachel rolled over on her bed and stared through the chink in the curtains. The sliver of sky she could see through the gap, was an exceedingly dark grey, but as the sun probably hadn't risen yet, that didn't necessarily signify another bleak day, weather-wise. Then she heard the tappity-tap of raindrops against the windowpane. Definitely raining again.

At least the electricity was back on, so that was something. She'd had to use the lanterns Holly and Gabriel had given her, to see to make a cup of coffee last night, using a saucepan to heat the water. And removing her make-up, what little she was wearing, and cleaning her teeth, had been interesting, to say the least. Several times she'd almost jumped out of her skins as shadows had leapt out of every corner. Candlelight and battery-lit lanterns may add an air of romance at certain times, but when you're alone in an otherwise dark cottage, with creaking floorboards and rattling windows, it isn't one of those times. The bedroom felt a whole lot cosier this morning with the bedside lamp glowing brightly.

'Yes, but that's the point,' Rachel said, with a sigh. 'Janet had obviously told them to behave like that. She told me to go upstairs and throw some water on my face to freshen up and when I came back down, only Holly was there. She linked her arm through mine and took me back out. I was dreading it, I can tell you but no one even so much as looked in my direction – except Lucas – and he only smiled, then quickly looked away and carried on chatting to Henry Goode, the farmer I told you about who moved that fallen tree.'

'It's all been happening in Hideaway Down, hasn't it? Just think, we both expected you to be lonely and bored and to be spending your first night curled up on a sofa, with a book. Instead you've got new friends. You've told them all about Drew and Jenny. You've had a little 'mini breakdown moment' – which everyone was good enough to let pass without comment, and you've had a candlelit dinner with a possible new love interest.'

'Lucas isn't a possible love interest, Sonia. Why does everyone keep saying that?'

'Actually, I meant the dog, Monty. From what you said about him, he's definitely taken a shine to you.'

'Oh, ha ha.'

'Who else said Lucas and you may have potential then?'

Rachel sighed. 'Holly, Ivy and Janet all thought he seemed... interested, but as I told them, we only met last night and we sort of got friendly due to the circumstances we were in, nothing else.'

'But you said you thought he was going to kiss you.'

Rachel tutted. 'Yes. I was probably mistaken though. Let's face it, I'm not good at judging what people actual mean, or feel, or intend. Drew proved that. Or perhaps it was just the candlelight and the storm and everything. Anyway, he didn't, so it's irrelevant.'

'Did you want him to?'

Rachel sat up and slid off the bed. She walked to the window and pulled open the curtains. Exceedingly dark grey sky, grey sea, rain... and a very wet animal, possibly a fox, or perhaps a dog, barely visible in the twilight, rolling over and over in the mud in the back garden of Ivy Cottage. Rachel peered through the rain-splattered glass. It was Monty. But where was Lucas and why was Monty in *her* garden and not in the garden of Mistletoe Cottage?

'Rachel?' Sonia said. 'I asked if you wanted him to kiss you. Are you still there? Hello?'

Rachel turned to face the phone. 'Sorry, Sonia. I'm still here... but I think I have to go. I've just looked out the window and Monty is rolling around in my garden with Lucas nowhere in sight. Do you think something may have happened to him? I'd better go and check.'

'Who? Lucas or the dog?'

Rachel tugged her T-shirt nightdress over her head, and tossing it on the bed, pulled on a pair of jeans and a jumper. 'Lucas, of course. Monty looks as if he's having the time of his life. Even though it's pouring hard and he's saturated and covered in mud.'

'Then what's the problem? Lucas probably let the dog out for a pee and, as it's raining, he stayed indoors. Sounds pretty sensible to me.'

'Maybe. But I don't think he would've just let Monty out to roam around, especially in the twilight. I told you that these cottages are on a cliff. In that picture on the website they look as if they're quite a distance away from the edge, but in reality, they're actually not that far. Holly told me that the cliff is being constantly eroded by the weather and the sea. I wouldn't be surprised to wake up on the beach one morning this week.'

'I've done that – but it had nothing to do with cliff erosion. It was more to do with a jug or two of Mojitos and a rather hot Spaniard. So what's the problem about Monty and the cliff?'

'Yes, I remember the photos on Facebook.' Rachel tutted, grabbed her phone and dashed towards the stairs. 'The problem with Monty and the cliff is, that if he makes his way to the edge, or chases something, it's a very long drop. In this dim light, the edge is probably difficult to see, and I don't think Monty's very bright at the best of times. Lovely, friendly mutt, but last in line when they handed out the intelligence gene, I suspect. He'd probably go straight over the edge. I saw how Lucas was with him last night. He adores that dog and believe me, he wouldn't take the risk of his beloved friend falling over a cliff edge. I've got to go.'

'Let me know what happens.'

'I will. I'll call you later. Bye.'

Rachel pressed 'end call', put on her walking boots, yanked her raincoat from the hook and headed towards the back door, slipping her arms into her coat as she walked. She'd make sure Monty was safe and then she'd go and see where Lucas was.

The moment she opened the door, Monty's ears shot up; he sat bolt upright and then bounded towards her. Wet muddy dog heading for woman wearing a bright yellow raincoat. Rachel realised too late, that she should've thought this through.

'Down, Monty! Down boy.' She tried to sound firm but Monty took about as much notice of her commands as he had of Lucas', yesterday evening.

She tugged at his collar and after what felt like going six rounds with the 2016 Olympics, champion wrestler, she finally got Monty to sit – even if it was on her feet. Thank heavens she'd put on her heavy-duty boots.

'You're a lump, do you know that? No! Don't you dare...'

Monty shook himself and, like a robot going berserk in a car paint spraying factory, globules of mud and water shot all over Rachel, and splattered against the kitchen walls and worktops.

'Oh great. Thanks very much, Monty.'

He barked as if to say: 'Don't mention it. It was my pleasure.'

She was sure she'd seen him smile, too. Or perhaps his lips were simply sticking to his teeth. Auntie Elsie's cat, Hortense did that. That cat seemed to have a permanent smirk on her pampered, furry face.

'Where's your master?'

Monty barked three times.

'Hmm. No idea what that means but hey, things are looking up. At least I'm talking to a dog now and not just to myself.'

He barked again and sat back down.

'Ow! Get off me, you hairy lump.' She laughed and dragged her feet from beneath his bulk. 'Okay. You stay here for a minute – and don't make a mess. Or should I say, any more mess?' She glanced at her watch. It was only seven-thirty. Well, either Lucas was up, or he wasn't, and if he wasn't, how had Monty got out? 'Stay,' she said, backing out of the kitchen into the hall and closing the door shut behind her.

She raced to the front door with the sound of Monty's barking, following her. She didn't want to take him with her to Mistletoe Cottage, just in case he got away from her and ended up in a worse predicament than when she'd 'rescued' him. And if – God forbid – something had happened to Lucas, she didn't want to have to deal with an emergency and a manic dog. Although what on earth could have possibly happened since she'd said a hurried goodnight to him last night, after Holly had driven them home from the pub, was beyond her comprehension.

The rain was easing off but it was still drizzling and by the time she stepped over the many puddles and made it to the door of Lucas' cottage, it was starting to get a little heavier once more.

She rang the bell, banged on the door and called Lucas' name through the letter box.

'A Goode, good morning to you,' a voice said, from behind her as she stepped from foot to foot, wondering what to do next. 'Terrible weather again.'

She glanced round. 'Oh. Hello, Harry.' She recognised him from The Snowdrop Inn last night. Lucas had spent at least half an hour drooling over Beatrix, Harry's girlfriend and a budding film star – although Lucas denied the drooling… and the amount of time, when Ivy mentioned it, later.

Harry was smiling but his expression turned to concern when Rachel spun around to face him.

'Did you fall over? You're covered in mud. Is everything okay?'

Rachel managed a smile. 'I'm fine, thanks. This was Monty's way of saying good morning. He's Lucas' dog, remember? I'm not sure if everything's okay though. I found him in my garden just now. Monty, not Lucas, obviously, but there's no sign of Lucas. I'm worried something's... Oh!'

The door of Mistletoe Cottage opened and Lucas stood on the threshold wearing only boxer shorts and a sleep-addled expression.

'Where's the fire?' He yawned, stretched and opened his eyes as wide as saucers. 'Christ! It's freezing.'

'Well, you're virtually naked,' Harry pointed out. 'A Goode, good morning, Lucas. Although from the look of you, I suspect it isn't.'

'Huh? Er. I've just woken up. What time is it? Was that you ringing the bell and thumping on my door, Harry? I know I forgot to leave a note about the milk but—'

'No,' Rachel interrupted, dragging her eyes away from Lucas' boxer shorts. 'It was me and it's just gone seven-thirty. Monty's in my kitchen. I thought something had happened to you.'

Lucas blinked several times as if he had only seen her that moment. He looked down at his state of undress and stepped back, grabbing a jacket from the coat rack, and shrugging it on.

'Sorry. Monty's what? In your kitchen? He can't be. He was upstairs in his bed the last time I saw him, and I've only opened the door to you. Don't tell me he's making you breakfast.' He grinned at his own joke. 'Sorry, that was a pathetic attempt at humour. Er. Are you serious?' He glanced back along the hall as if expecting his dog to appear at any moment.

'Yes. I left him there in case I couldn't keep hold of him. He's built like a bear. Not that I know what a bear's built like. I've never seen one in the flesh. I've always wanted to though.'

'Huh?' Lucas and Harry said, simultaneously.

'Nothing.' Rachel coughed to hide her embarrassment. She did go on about the silliest things sometimes. Drew was always telling her that she went off on a tangent. 'Anyway, are you coming to get him or do you want to give me his lead so that I can bring him to you? And will you please decide quickly because you may not have noticed but it's raining.'

'Oh God. Sorry. Come in.'

'I don't want to come in, thanks. I've got to clean the kitchen. It's a complete mess. I just want to know what to do about Monty.'

'I'm guessing the mess has something to do with him.' Lucas pulled a face. 'And so does the state of your coat. I'll pay to have it cleaned.'

'It has everything to do with him, but it's only mud, so it'll wash off. The kitchen and my coat, hopefully.'

'Then give me five minutes to get dressed and I'll come and get him and help you clean up. But I've got no idea how he got out. Where was he? I'm assuming you didn't find him in your kitchen – unless there's a secret tunnel between the two cottages and Monty discovered it.'

Harry laughed. 'There's a secret tunnel in The Snowdrop Inn. Used to be used by the smugglers in the olden days. Don't know of one up here though. These places were only built in the 1840s, I think. How many bottles of milk d'you want, Lucas?'

'Er. One, please. No. Better make that two. I think

72

I'm going to need a lot of coffee this morning. Gabriel and I carried on drinking when we got back last night. He was picking my brains – what little there is of them – for his new book. His hero is an architect. What are the chances of that?'

'No way!' Harry said. 'That's awesome. Perhaps he'll name him after you.'

Lucas grinned. 'I don't think I'm really hero material, and besides, he's already named him. He's called Marcus.'

From where Rachel was standing, Lucas looked very much like her idea of a hero; a hero who had just got out of bed after a long night of scorching hot sex, but she instantly dismissed the notion.

'Sorry guys. Raining, remember?' she said, pointing upwards. Raindrops were now beginning to bounce off Harry's shoulders as well as hers, not to mention the path. Surely, she shouldn't have had to remind either of them of the fact?

'Sorry, Rachel!' Lucas said. 'You go back to your place and I'll come round as soon as I'm dressed. No point in having a shower first, if I know Monty and his ability to make a mess.'

'How many bottles for you, Rachel?' Harry asked, grinning. 'Don't worry, I'll bring them to your door.'

'Um. Two, please. I think Lucas isn't the only one who'll be needing a lot of coffee today. I'll get the empty one from yesterday.'

She ran down the path, avoiding as many of the puddles as she could and arrived at the door of Ivy Cottage just as the rain turned into another heavy downpour. She couldn't help but smile as she closed the door behind her, though. Seeing Lucas in his boxer shorts had made her morning. She began to wonder what he'd look like out of them – until a crash and a whimper, from the direction of the kitchen brought her back to her senses.

What had Monty done now?

Chapter Nine

'Come in,' Rachel yelled, hearing the doorbell and assuming it was Lucas. 'It's open.'

'It's me.' Harry Goode called from the hall. 'I've brought your milk.'

Rachel had already forgotten about that. 'Sorry, Harry. Be with you in a tick. Or you can come through.'

Harry strolled into the kitchen and his eyes opened wide in disbelief when he saw the walls decorated with mud. 'Wow! How many dogs did you say did this?'

'Tell me about it,' Rachel said, struggling to hold Monty.

'Do you need a hand?'

'I'm trying to remove a chip of china from this stupid dog's paw but he won't hold still. Is Lucas far behind you?'

Harry shook his head. 'Don't know. He went to get dressed. How did the dog get a bit of china in his paw?'

'I'm assuming he knocked the mug that was on the draining board off onto the floor, where it smashed to smithereens on these granite tiles, or whatever they are.' She nodded her head towards the jigsaw-like pieces of mug scattered across the floor, together with a saucepan and a spoon. 'When I came in after hearing the crash, he was limping and I can see a trace of blood. Do you think you could see the underside of his paw if I can hold him still for as long as one second?'

'Saved by the bell,' Harry said, as the doorbell rang again. 'Come in, Lucas,' he yelled. 'It's open.' He smiled at Rachel. 'I assume you wanted him to.'

She managed a smile but as Lucas entered the kitchen, Monty leapt out of Rachel's grip, sending her flying backwards. The resounding crack to her head sent a spasm of pain searing through her.

'Rachel!'

The panic in Lucas' voice seemed far off in the distance and even Monty's barking floated away to nothing. Hundreds of stars flashed in front of her eyes. Lucas' voice grew momentarily louder as he repeated her name and anxiously asked if she was okay. But she couldn't answer. She seemed to be cosseted in a warm, dark blanket, or something. Whatever it was, it was wrapping around her, firmly but gently. She was floating through the air… and all the lights went out.

They came back on moments later, when she opened her eyes and blinked several times.

'Oh. I thought there'd been another power cut. Ow!' Her hand shot to the back of her head.

'No. You passed out.' The relief in Lucas' voice was apparent. 'But only for a second or two, thank God. Are you okay?'

'I think so. Did I really pass out?'

'Yep,' Harry said. 'I'll make you a cup of tea. That'll make you feel better – at least that's what my mum always says. Tea cures everything according to her. Even a fractured skull.'

'Oh my God! I don't have a fractured skull, do I?' The only thing she could feel was a rather large lump, and it seemed to be growing in size as she touched it.

'I was joking.' Harry looked apologetic. 'Sorry. Didn't mean to panic you.'

'I think it sounded worse than it was,' Lucas said. 'You gave us quite a scare for a moment. Sit and take it easy for a while.'

Even his eyes appeared to be smiling as he tilted his head a fraction and scanned her face – although perhaps Rachel was just imagining that due to the knock to her head.

She realised she was sitting in the armchair in front of the Range but had no idea how she got there. Lucas must have carried her.

'Here. Drink this.'

Harry handed her a cup of tea which she dutifully sipped. It was sweet, no doubt full of sugar, but nevertheless, it was most welcome. She smiled at Monty who was sitting to one side of where Lucas was crouched beside her. Monty's head was also tilted slightly and he held one paw in the air. Rachel sat bolt upright but wished she hadn't. She squinted as a dart of pain shot through her shoulder, and a wave of tea slopped into her lap. 'Monty's paw,' she said, ignoring the warm wet patch on her jeans and pointing at the raised paw. 'He's got a piece of broken china in it. I was trying to get it out when you came in.'

Lucas' head whipped round so that he could look at his dog. 'Let me see, boy.'

Without so much as a whimper, Monty held his paw higher and Lucas bent further forward and examined it.

'Got ya!' After a moment or two of poking and pulling, Lucas held a large sliver of china between his fingers. 'I think there's a song about holding china in your hand,' he joked.

'Don't give up the day job, my friend,' Harry said, patting him on the shoulder. 'D'you need a hand clearing this place up? My milk round's not quite over, but I'm sure they won't mind waiting. Or I can finish and come back.'

'Don't worry,' Lucas said. 'This also looks far worse than it is. I'm used to clearing up messes like this. It'll only take me thirty minutes or so.'

Rachel moved forward to stand up.

'What do you think you're doing?' Lucas asked.

'I'm going to help.'

'No you're not. You're going to sit there and drink your tea. I'm sure you're fine but you need to rest for a while. I'm just going to take Monty outside and wash some of the mud off him, or he'll wait until I've got the kitchen spotless and shake another batch all over the place.'

'But I—'

'Please don't argue, Rachel. I'm skilled at this. And it is my fault, after all. I discovered how he got out. I took him out for a final pee last night after I left Holly and Gabriel's, and I didn't shut the back door properly. The latch hadn't caught and I hadn't drawn the bolt across, so all Monty had to do was ease it open and voilà! Doggy freedom. I'll make sure I check it at least three times before I go to bed every night from now on.'

'I'll love you and leave you then, if you're sure you don't need me,' Harry said. 'Have a Goode, good day, all.'

'Thanks, Harry,' Rachel and Lucas said in unison, accompanied by a goodbye bark from Monty.

'I assume there's a bucket in one of these cupboards,' Lucas said, looking first in the one beneath the sink. 'Ta dah!' He held up a bright orange bucket before Rachel had time to reply, and filled it with water. 'I'll give him a proper shower later, but this'll get the worst off. Come on, boy.' Lucas led Monty outside, and with a final smile at Rachel, he closed the door firmly behind him.

Chapter Ten

'I wonder who that is...' Rachel nodded her head in the direction of a slightly overweight man on his way to the front door of Vine Cottage. He had a holdall tossed over one shoulder and was moving in a way that Rachel could only describe as 'strutting'.

She, Lucas and Monty were going to drive to the village and Lucas was treating her to breakfast in The Coffee Hideaway. Lucas had insisted. It was a way to say sorry for the mess Monty had caused, and also to thank her for rescuing Monty in the first place, he'd told her. It had taken him about half an hour to clean up the mud in the kitchen, after which he'd taken Monty back to Mistletoe Cottage so that both he and his dog could have showers. By the time they'd returned to Ivy Cottage, the rain had stopped. Rachel was starving, so she'd happily agreed.

'He doesn't look like a rock star, that's for sure,' Lucas said, glancing at the stranger. 'Didn't Gabriel or someone say something about a singer coming to stay? Or did I imagine that?'

'I think someone did say that, but perhaps they were

joking. It was when we were saying how odd it was that so many 'famous' people seemed to have moved to Hideaway Down.'

'Morning,' Rachel said with a smile and a wave as they drew level with the man, although they were separated by the pathway and garden of Mistletoe Cottage.

The man waved back, removing earbuds from his ears as he did so. 'Morning, love, Morning, mate. Bleeding awful weather. Unless you're a duck. You staying in that one?' He nodded his head towards Ivy Cottage and beamed at them. 'Romantic weekend, is it? Or you here for the week? Heard there was a power cut last night. Bet that was fun.' He winked, making his meaning abundantly clear.

'We didn't come here together,' Rachel said rather too quickly. 'We only met last night.'

That made the man smile even more. 'I've come to the right place then. I could do with a bit of romance myself. Seen any single women around my age – late fifties but young at heart, if you get my drift. Or were you too busy getting to know one another to notice anyone else?'

He winked again and Rachel wondered if he had something wrong with his eye; a nervous twitch perhaps, although he definitely didn't look the nervous type. More the cocky, Jack-the-lad sort.

'I'm Rachel, this is Lucas and that's Monty.' She pointed towards the car park area where Monty was heading at considerable speed. 'And we're here for the week.'

'We arrived last night,' Lucas added.

'Happy to meet you. I'm Billy. Billy Brookes. Here for two weeks. Old friend of mine recommended this place. I hate hotels. Like to have my own space and a bit

81

of good clean fresh air, not bleeding air conditioning. That dog of yours looks like he's got a hot date.'

Lucas grinned. 'I promised him a fresh bone from the local butcher, not that he deserves it.'

'Bit of a lad, is he?'

'You could say that.'

'So, you off to the village? Just drove through it. Looks like something you'd see on the telly as the setting for one of those cosy murder mysteries. Pub looks like my sort of watering hole though and it's owned by the woman who owns these. Wonder if we get a discount. Hope the grub's good. Don't know one end of a frying pan from the other, so I'll be eating out.'

'Janet's lovely,' Rachel said. 'And so is The Snowdrop Inn. We didn't try the food but what I saw looked delicious.'

'And come to think of it,' Lucas said. 'Janet's in her early fifties, I would say, and I'm pretty sure she's single. Good-looking too, especially for her age.'

'Lucas!' Rachel glared at him when he glanced round at her. He had the decency to look apologetic.

'Yeah?' Billy sounded keen. 'I assumed she'd be hitched. If she's anything like her daughter, she'll be a stunner. That Holly's a bit of all right, isn't she? Too young for me though. I like my women to have been around the block a few times, if you know what I mean? I'll dump my stuff and take a look then. Ta for that. See you later. I'll buy you a pint if you're in the pub.'

He shoved his earbuds back in place and increased the pace of his strut.

'I'm not sure Janet will thank you for that,' Rachel said quietly, although Billy probably couldn't hear her with his music in his ears. She wondered what he was listening to.

'He looks harmless, but you're right. I shouldn't have

82

said that. I'm not sure what came over me.'

'Testosterone, I suspect. You were doing a bit of the old 'male bonding'.'

He grinned and nudged her with his elbow. 'I heard you all discussing how hot Jamie McDay looked in his vampire outfit last night, and how lucky Laurel thought she was to have him. So don't pretend you women aren't just as bad when it comes to the opposite sex.'

'Okay. I'll give you that. But as we all told Laurel, Jamie's lucky to have her, too.'

'He is,' Lucas replied. 'He told us that meeting Laurel was the best thing that had ever happened to him – and all because he wanted a decent cup of coffee. That's how they met.'

'I know. Laurel told me the whole story. She was madly in love with Ned at the time, but he, of course, was head over heels in love with Ivy.'

'And even more so now that they're expecting. I don't think I've ever seen a man more excited at the prospect of fatherhood than Ned Stelling was last night.'

'Wait until he has to get up at two in the morning to soothe a crying baby, and when he has to change a nappy or clear up vomit. I wonder if he'll be so thrilled then.'

'That sounds a bit cynical.' Lucas gave her an odd look. 'Not all men find that a problem. I've done those things several times and I didn't mind at all. And—'

'You…you've got kids?' Rachel stopped in her tracks. She could feel the colour draining from her face and for a split second, she actually thought she might throw up. How bizarre was that? But he hadn't mentioned kids last night. Not once. And for some peculiar reason, this was a bolt out of the blue.

He stopped too and turned to face her, giving her a searching look.

'A nephew and a niece. And I was going to say,

83

you're forgetting all the bonuses, like hearing them laugh and seeing their smiles. Seeing them walk for the first time, or hearing them say their first words. Are you okay, Rachel? You've gone really pale.'

A wave of relief swept over her. A nephew and a niece. Thank you, God, thank you. She smiled and continued walking. 'I'm fine. Just very, very hungry. And look how patiently Monty is sitting beside your car!'

'There's a first time for everything.' Lucas fell into step beside her and unlocked the car with the remote.

He held the passenger door open for Rachel, but Monty jumped in before her and sat on the front seat, peering ahead as if he were oblivious to the fact that he wasn't supposed to be there.

Rachel burst out laughing.

Lucas tutted and pointed a finger towards the back seat. 'Get in the back please, Monty.'

With the merest of whimpers, Monty leapt over the seat, yawned and stretched out across the full-length of the rear seat.

Lucas looked a little surprised that his dog had actually done what he'd asked.

'I could've sat in the back,' Rachel said, giggling.

'It's covered in dog's hair. But then so is the front seat now. Hold on.' He brushed several strands of fur off the seat, using the sleeve of his jacket.

'You seemed surprised that Monty obeyed your command,' Rachel said, getting into the car when Lucas stepped back.

'I'm astonished. But miracles do happen, it seems.' He closed the passenger door, dashed round to the driver's side and got in.

Rachel watched him click the seat belt in place and turn on the ignition. He looked directly at her and smiled

84

before easing the car out onto Hideaway Hill.
'They certainly do,' she said.
But she hadn't meant to say it out loud.

Chapter Eleven

Ivy slumped into the leather, winged chair opposite her grandfather in the private snug of The Snowdrop Inn, and let out a long, troubled sigh.

'How's the lovely Sarah, Gramps? Are you seriously thinking of marrying her?'

Gordon eyed her over his reading glasses, closed his book and placed it on the small table beside him. Leaning back in his chair, he smiled lovingly. 'Don't you want me to, sweetheart?'

Ivy's head shot up from her chest. 'Of course I do. If it's what you want. Everyone deserves to be happy, Gramps, especially you.'

'Why, "especially" me? I'm no angel. But everyone does deserve to find happiness, you're right about that.'

'And Sarah makes you happy? Really, truly, happy?'

He nodded. 'She does. I hope I do the same for her.'

'You make everyone happy. You were always there for Holly, me and Mum, no matter what. Even when Gran got sick. Do you miss her? Gran, I mean.'

'Every single day. But she's here in my heart and always will be.' He tapped his chest and smiled again. 'It doesn't mean I can't love someone else though. Sarah will never replace your gran. No one ever could.' He sat forward and reached for Ivy's hand. 'What's this about, sweetheart? I have a feeling it's less to do with me and Sarah Saltcote and more to do with you and Ned. Is something wrong? Has something happened?'

Ivy grinned. 'How did you get to be so smart?'

'Old age. So what's the problem then?'

Ivy took his hand and smoothed out the wrinkles on his skin with her thumb.

'It'll take more than your thumb to get rid of those,' he quipped. 'Now come on, child. Tell your grandpa what ails you.'

'I'm just being silly. I know I am. Ned loves me and he was over the moon when I told him about the babies.'

'But?'

She met his eyes and smiled. 'But... I'm a walking disaster, Gramps. We all know that. What if I do something wrong? What if Ned stops loving me? What if he leaves me a few years down the line? What if...'

Gramps squeezed her fingers. 'What if he does to you what your dad did to your mum, you mean? Ivy, listen to me. This is simply your hormones. Don't give me that look. Bethany Morrison – this year's May Queen, passes on all her old magazines to Sarah and she reads them out to me.'

'I know who Bethany Morrison is. She's the girl with the ring through her nose.' Ivy grinned. 'But you're seriously telling me that Sarah reads out articles from magazines like Cosmo? Sarah Saltcote?'

He nodded. 'My Sarah. She's not as stuffy as you think, sweetheart, once you really get to know her. As I was saying, it's your hormones. Because your mum and your dad were childhood sweethearts, and you've known Ned since you were old enough to pull his hair – yes, you used to do that. I saw you more than once. You always wanted to be in charge.'

'Nothing's changed. Except I don't pull his hair. Well, I do but only... oops. Sorry, Gramps. Too much information. You don't want to know about that.'

He tutted but patted her hand. 'Where was I? Oh yes, childhood sweethearts. Your mum and dad had twins. Now you and Ned are having twins. But the similarity ends there. Your father ran off with an ex. Ned's loved you all his life, even if he didn't want to admit it to himself or anyone else. And forgive me for saying this, but your dad is a bit of a berk.'

Ivy smiled. 'You're forgiven. I agree, he is.'

'Ned isn't. Ned's got his head screwed on.'

'But his dad left, too. Well, okay he died, and shortly after Ned was born, but everyone says he would've left if he had lived.'

'Or Audrey might've killed him, although she's probably too God-fearing to do that. The thing is, Ivy, we don't have to turn out like our parents and our lives don't have to be a repeat of theirs. Yes, you do sometimes do some silly things, but now you've got Ned and he'll look after you. I think he's one of the most reliable, dependable men I know. And Gabriel, of course. And look at him and Holly. Do you think he'll run off and leave her like that twit Paul did?'

'No. I think Holly and Gabriel are like swans – they'll mate for life, now they've found each other.'

'And so will you and Ned.'

'Then why hasn't he asked me to marry him?'

'What?'

'Why hasn't he asked me to be his wife? You're right about him. He is reliable, he is dependable, and trustworthy and kind and... and all those other things that make him so perfect, and now he's going to be a dad, so why hasn't he said we should get married?'

'Er. I think you're asking the wrong person, sweetheart. I think you should be having this conversation with Ned. But if you want my opinion and you're going to get it whether you want it or not, I suspect he's worried you may not want to. Don't forget, it wasn't that long ago that he thought you'd fallen for someone else. The poor man still thinks you can do better than him and it's taking a little while to get used to the idea that you want him, him and only him. Besides, you always made your views on marriage very clear. You didn't want anything to do with it.'

'Yes but that was before Ned and me got together. Before I knew that I wanted to spend the rest of my life with him. Before these two.' She rubbed her tummy.

'Well, you like being in charge, sweetheart. Why don't you propose to him?'

Ivy's eyes opened wide. 'I like that idea, Gramps. But what if he says no?'

Gramps let out a long, exasperated sigh. 'Well now, Ivy, you're just being plain stupid. There's more chance of me and Sarah dancing naked down Market Street than there is of Ned Stelling saying no to you. Say no, indeed. I've never heard anything so ridiculous in my life.'

'Have I told you recently how much I love you, Gramps?'

'No. So tell me now. Then get out of here. But come back and fill me in on your plans for your big proposal... that is, once you, Holly and your mum have finalised them.'

Chapter Twelve

Out of the corner of her eye Janet Gilroy spotted the stranger making a beeline for the bar. She knew she hadn't seen him before and yet there was something about him that seemed so... So... what? Familiar? Comforting? Homely. That was it. He was smiling at her and she felt as if she were wrapped up in her favourite dressing gown, sipping a glass of wine in front of a roaring fire. How strange. She couldn't take her gaze from him, and when he reached the bar, his smile widened and his deep blue eyes twinkled with something akin to delight.

'You must be Janet,' the man said. 'You look just like your daughter Holly but if I didn't know better I'd think you were her sister not her mum.'

Janet had heard that line a thousand times and yet from his lips, it almost sounded sincere. She tried not to look flattered, but she knew she failed as her cheeks burned and her lips unwittingly curved into a wide smile.

'And you are?' She managed a sliver of ice in her tone.

He held out his hand and she instinctively took it, intending to shake it in a business-like fashion. To her surprise, he twisted his hand, and lifted hers to his lips, softly brushing her fingers in a gentle kiss. She quickly pulled herself free as a skin-tingling wave of electricity shot through her.

'Billy Brookes. I'm the lucky chappie who's spending the next two weeks in your lovely Vine Cottage, and from what I've seen so far, I'm looking forward to mingling a bit of business with a lot of pleasure.'

'Oh.' Janet wasn't usually lost for words but today was an exception. 'What type of business are you in?'

'Property. There's a couple of places over in Eastbourne that've taken my fancy, so I've come to have a better look at the area in general.'

'Investment? Buy to let? Or refurbish and sell on?'

He beamed at her. 'The first and the third. Buy to let is too much hassle.'

'Fascinating. Do you want a drink? Or did you just come in to introduce yourself?'

He winked. 'Both. I'll have a pint of whatever you recommend, please, and have one yourself.'

'Thanks. But I don't drink pints.'

'Now you know that's not what I meant. You have whatever you like.'

Janet tried not to smile, but his cheeky grin was contagious.

'Not while I'm working, but thanks for the offer.'

'That's okay. I'll buy you a drink when you're not working. When's your next night off?'

'Oh. Er... I own the place. I don't get nights off.' She tried to hide her surprise.

He glanced down the length of the bar. 'You've got staff. I'm sure they could cope without you for a couple of hours. But if you don't think they're up to it, we could have a drink here.' He winked again and grinned. 'Come on, Janet. Say yes to a lonely builder.'

'Builder? You're a builder?'

'First and foremost, although I've got a team who do most of the hard graft these days. I've never had that reaction before, when I've told a lovely lady like yourself my occupation. Normally, their eyes glaze over. Got a thing for builders, have you? Not that I'm complaining. Does that mean you'll have a drink with me?'

Janet smiled, rested her forearms on the bar and leant forward. 'Definitely. You have no idea how long I've been trying to find myself a builder. Do you have plans for tonight?'

Billy placed his forearms opposite her and leant forward, their faces only inches apart.

'A few are popping into my head right now.'

'And mine,' Janet said. 'Can you be here at seven?'

'On the dot.'

'Fabulous. I'll reserve one of my more secluded tables.'

'I like the sound of that.'

Janet smiled. 'I'll get you that beer, Billy. And it's on the house.' She turned and came face to face with Ivy. 'Oh, hello darling. I didn't see you there.'

Ivy grabbed her arm and pulled her towards the other end of the bar.

'You do realise that guy thinks he's going on a date with you, don't you? He hasn't a clue that when you said you've been looking for a builder you actually meant to do some building work. He may not be so pleased when he realises that your plans are paper and ink drawings of your proposed refurbishment of upstairs, and not *plans* for a romantic evening together.'

Janet kissed Ivy on her cheek. 'Needs must, darling. At this point in time I don't care what I have to do to get a builder upstairs.'

'Mum! Be careful what you say. He's a total stranger

and you don't know how he may react when he discovers you're leading him on.'

'Who says I'm leading him on? He's not bad looking and he's got a rather cheeky smile. And those eyes! It's been a long time since a man's looked at me like that. It sent shivers to places I'd forgotten existed, I can tell you.'

'Oh good God, Mum. Kill me now.'

Janet pulled Billy's pint. 'Don't you want your mum to have some fun, darling?'

'Yes, of course I do.'

'We'll don't worry then. Because that's exactly what I intend to do. And who says you can't mix business with pleasure?'

Ivy shook her head. 'I hope you know what you're doing. And when you've got a minute, I need to have a word with you.'

'If it's about the birds and bees, been there, done that.' Janet nudged her daughter's arm.

'No, Mum. I'm going to propose to Ned and I want to run a few things by you.' Ivy jumped back. 'Mum! You're spilling the beer.'

'Bugger!' Janet said, flicking the beer tap shut. Had her daughter really just told her that she was planning to propose to Ned?

This day was getting better by the minute.

Chapter Thirteen

'Hello, Janet,' Rachel said, leaning on the bar of The Snowdrop Inn, and stifling a yawn. 'Is it always this packed in here on a Sunday, or is it because it's pouring again?'

Janet positively beamed.

'Less to do with the weather and more to do with our famous Sunday lunch,' she said. 'I see you're with the lovely Lucas again this morning. Late night, was it?'

Rachel glanced over her shoulder to where Lucas was seated at a table near the window overlooking the pond, and smiled. Monty was already curled up on his master's feet, with one eye closed and the other looking in Rachel's direction.

'Yes,' she said. 'But unfortunately not for the reason you're implying. After we left here, we all went back to Holly Cottage and had a few more drinks. Well, the others did. I drank coffee because one more glass of wine and I'd have been on the floor.'

'I know that feeling,' Janet said.

'So do I. Gabriel wanted to ask Lucas a little more about his profession, for his new book and I tagged along because Holly invited me in. I should've simply gone home to bed because yesterday was a very long day.'

'Starting off with Lucas' dog making the kitchen look like a hippo's watering hole, I'm told.'

'Oh. You heard about that?'

Janet grinned. 'You're in Hideaway Down. Nothing stays secret here for long.'

'It's all cleaned up. Lucas made it spotless. And only one mug got broken.'

'Don't worry about it, Rachel. Far worse things have happened in those cottages, believe me.' Janet was still grinning as she stacked clean glasses on a shelf behind her, looking over her shoulder at Rachel. 'Then you went for breakfast at Laurel's, I hear.'

'Wow! You weren't joking, were you? Who told you that?'

'Meg Stanbridge saw you.' Janet turned and met Rachel's eye. 'To quote her very words: "Saw that pretty, young Rachel and that nice Lucas, and that big furry dog, in The Coffee Hideaway, I did. Bright and early. Looked much happier, she did. They make a lovely couple, they do." I've got one of those memories that can recall almost anything I hear. Drives me nuts sometimes. And yet funnily enough, I never seem to be able to remember the things I really want to.'

Rachel smiled. 'Well, after breakfast, we drove into Eastbourne and looked around the shops. Then we took Monty up to Beachy Head. But it was raining and Lucas had to keep him on the lead because there's no fencing or anything and that really is a long way down, so we didn't stay long. Is it true that people have fallen off? Lucas said a couple of foreign students have.'

Janet nodded. 'It's true. They get too close to the edge and over they go. It used to be a popular spot for suicides too, but not so much these days. It's very sad, whether by choice or by accident but there are plenty of warning signs and they now even have rangers patrolling the cliff.'

'It's beautiful up there. But it's just as good a view up on Hideaway Cliff.'

'And just as big a drop. What did you do after that?'

'You haven't heard?' Rachel didn't think Janet would be offended by a little sarcasm.

'Sometimes it takes a while for word to get through.' Janet winked, so she obviously found it amusing.

'Well, we went back to the cottages to change, and then we came straight here.'

'Ah. I haven't missed much then.'

'Um.' Rachel fiddled with her purse. 'How was your night, if you don't mind me asking? I thought I saw you in here having dinner with the guy staying in Vine Cottage, and Holly said later that you were on a date with him. Billy, isn't it?' Much to Rachel's surprise, Janet blushed. 'Sorry, Janet. It's none of my business. I must stop saying out loud whatever pops into my head.'

Janet smiled. 'It's not a problem. I asked you enough about your love life on Friday night, and I've heard all about your day, so I suppose it's only fair that you know about mine.' She folded her arms and leant on the bar. 'But I wouldn't call it a date, exactly. We discussed some building work I've needed done for a considerable time. Builders are like gold dust, did you know that? You can't find one for love nor money, no matter how hard you search. Then just like that, there's one right under your nose.' She leant further forward and lowered her voice. 'And when he's got a cheeky grin and a twinkle in his eyes, well, that's a bonus.' She winked and straightened up. 'Watch this space, is all I'll say. Now what can I get you? Are you here for Sunday lunch?'

Rachel laughed. 'Yes. We were told it's the best for miles around. Two roast beefs with all the trimmings, please. And is there any chance of Monty having any leftover scraps? Holly said there might be.'

'Yep. I always keep a few leftovers for my more discerning canine customers. I'll have them brought over with your meals. Bottle of wine?'

'Red, please.'

'Coming right up.'

Chapter Fourteen

Ivy smiled up at Rachel from the stool in front of Janet's dressing table mirror.

'Are you sure you don't mind doing this?' Ivy asked. 'I could leave it until tomorrow. The hair salons in Eastbourne will be open then and I'm sure one of them will be able to squeeze me in.'

Rachel returned her smile. 'Not at all. I'm happy to help,' she said, and she meant it. Just as she had when Ivy had stopped her as she and Lucas were leaving The Snowdrop Inn after Sunday lunch. "I only want a quick trim," Ivy had said, and knowing that Rachel was a hairdresser, she had thought there was no harm in asking. "I'm happy to pay you, of course," Ivy added, to which Rachel had replied that there was really no need for that and that she'd happily cut Ivy's hair. So at six p.m. sharp, Rachel had returned to the pub, as requested.

'I'm really nervous,' Ivy said. 'Oh, not about you cutting my hair, Rachel. About proposing to Ned.'

'What's the rush?' Holly asked, sprawled out across Janet's bed. 'Ned's not going anywhere. Why do you need to propose to him this evening? Why don't you do it on Friday or Saturday? Take him somewhere nice for dinner. Somewhere far away from Hideaway Down so that there won't be anyone watching your every move and reporting back to the rest of the village.'

'I want to do it today. I want him to marry me and the sooner I ask, the sooner we can all start planning the wedding.'

'Just imagine if he says no.'

Holly rolled onto her back as Ivy twisted on her stool and threw one of Janet's hairbrushes at her sister.

'That's not funny,' Ivy said. 'You may be surprised to hear this, but that's actually what I'm afraid of. What if he does say no? I mean, I don't think he will, but what if he does?'

Holly swung her legs around and slid off the bed, retrieving the hairbrush from the floor and handing it to Rachel, who placed it back on the dressing table.

'Don't be so stupid, Ivy.' Holly walked to the window and looked out. 'There's absolutely no chance of Ned saying no. He's been in love with you all his life. I don't know what's come over you lately. You never used to be this... needy, or lacking in confidence. You always used to be so sure of yourself. Mum says that you've changed since the accident, but I think it started before that. I think it started when you realised just how madly in love you were with Ned. It came as a bit of a shock, didn't it?'

'You can say that again.' Ivy glanced up at Rachel, via the mirror. 'You didn't know me before I started dating Ned, Rachel, but believe me, I was a completely different girl. I drove like a maniac, drank like a fish, burnt the candle, not just at both ends, but in the middle too, and lived for my job. I worked in the music business, and I organised the lives and careers of many of the singers, bands and musicians who are now household names.'

'But she gave it all up for *lurve*,' Holly said, with an

air of drama. 'Do you know, it's still bloody well raining? I wouldn't be surprised if Meg Stanbridge or one of the others, starts suggesting we build an ark.'

'Not Meg,' Ivy said. 'She'd only be allowed to take two geese, and there's no way she'd leave any of the Gaggle Gang behind.'

'Did you really give it all up for love?' Rachel asked, continuing combing and cutting section after section of Ivy's lustrous auburn locks. 'You've got incredibly beautiful hair, you know.' She glanced at Holly. 'You both have.'

'Thanks,' Ivy and Holly said simultaneously.

'And yes I did,' Ivy added. 'Give it all up for love. But not because Ned asked me to or anything. I got drunk after a... misunderstanding with Ned and very, very stupidly decided to drive my car. I only went a few feet before I crashed it into a lamppost, nearly killing one of the Gaggle Gang in the process. No one was hurt, apart from me, and I was only slightly injured. Ned got me out of the car and... well, it was a bit of a wake-up call. I did lose my licence though, quite rightly.'

'Oh God. How awful.'

Ivy nodded. 'It could've been so much worse. The thing is, falling in love with Ned really took me by surprise. I lived in London and only came home for the occasional weekend and high days and holidays. I wanted to travel the world. I loved excitement and variety. I really didn't see myself coming back to Hideaway Down to live. After the accident, I suddenly knew there was nowhere else I would rather be. And no one else I would rather be with. So a few months later, I told Ned I was coming home, and he asked me to move in with him.' She rubbed her tummy. 'I hadn't exactly planned on getting pregnant though. This is – typical me – another accident. Except this one, we're both very happy about.'

'Wow!' Rachel said. 'Isn't it funny how life rarely seems to turn out as we expect it to? After Drew and I started dating, I think I thought I would be with him forever. I got that completely wrong, didn't I?'

'Ah,' Ivy said. 'But now you've met the rather luscious Lucas.'

'Yes,' said Holly. 'And as Mum always says: "Anything can happen in Hideaway Down." Perhaps this was all meant to be.'

Rachel smiled at both of them. 'I really like Lucas, but it's far too early to know whether anything will come of it. We're simply two single people having fun. He hasn't even asked me out. Well, not as in: "Will you go out on a date with me, Rachel?" So I'm trying not to see too much into it just yet.'

'What will be, will be,' Holly said.

'There.' Rachel stepped back from Ivy. 'I've finished. You're ready to go.'

'Thanks so much, Rachel,' Ivy said. 'I know it's silly, but I always feel so much better when I know I haven't got any split ends.'

'Right.' Holly grabbed a bottle of red, sparkly nail polish from Janet's dressing table. 'Let's get your fingers and toes done and then I'll get Mum up here to do your make-up. She's so much better at it than us. And once that's done, you're ready to pop the question.'

Ivy smiled nervously. 'God. I really hope Ned says yes.'

'Of course he will,' Rachel and Holly said in unison.

'If you were prepared to wait a couple of weeks or so,' Holly added. 'I'm pretty certain that Ned would propose to you.'

'Perhaps. But I want to do this, Holly. I want Ned to know that I really want to marry him, so much so, that

101

I'm prepared to get down on my knees and ask him to spend the rest of his life with me. But if he does say no. He's dead. I'm telling you that for nothing.'

The three of them burst out laughing.

Even Rachel was certain Ned would accept, and it made her happy to feel that she had, in some small way, been a part of this next step in Ivy and Ned's relationship.

Chapter Fifteen

Ivy had never felt this nervous in her entire life. It was ridiculous and she knew it but her heart was racing, her palms were damp and her stomach felt as though she had swallowed a washing machine – although that could have been more to do with the tiny occupants in her womb than feeling nervous about asking Ned to marry her.

Her mum, her sister, Gramps, even Rachel were certain of the outcome of this evening, and if anyone had asked her a few weeks ago, she herself would have replied with a resounding: 'Of course he'll say yes.' But even the most confident people in life sometimes have niggling little doubts. Don't they?

Ivy took a deep breath, pushed her shoulders back and stood tall in her black stilettos. Her soft sheen, barely-there, black stockings were a trifle damp, and glancing down at the surrounding puddles and rain splashing onto her shoes, she wished she had taken Holly's advice to wear wellingtons from the pub to the smithy – where Ned had said he'd be at seven, when she'd asked him – and to change into her patent heels at Ned's door. It was too late now though, and besides, if things went to plan, she wouldn't be wearing her shoes or stockings for very much longer. In fact, she shouldn't be wearing anything for long, if it all went well – other than a massive smile on her perfectly made-up face.

She licked her glossy *Devil's Juice* lipstick-covered lips and primped her freshly trimmed hair with the fingers of her left hand – a hand that would very soon be wearing a token of her and Ned's commitment to one another – she hoped.

She shoved open the stable door of the smithy with her shoulder and stepped inside, turning around to close her umbrella and to slip off her raincoat. She hung both of them on the hooks beside the door before turning back to face the room. Only then did she see how the forge had been transformed and her jaw dropped so far and so fast that she wouldn't be surprised if it hit the floor like some character in a cartoon.

'Oh. My. Good. God!'

Ned, who was wearing the grey suit he had bought for Petunia and Bartram's wedding in August, and the baby-blue shirt and blue and grey tie Ivy had chosen to go with it, stood beneath a wrought iron arch, clearly crafted by his own hand, and threaded through with several dozen red roses. Behind him, his forge burned brightly despite the fact that he hadn't been working today. He had obviously prepared it especially for tonight and it was surrounded by glowing candles. The floor between him and Ivy was scattered with rose petals and to one side was a bistro table and two chairs. The table bore two covered silver platters, a bottle of champagne in an ice bucket and two glistening champagne saucers. To the other side, was a pile of exceptionally comfy-looking cushions and a faux fur rug topped with a matching faux fur blanket.

Ned smiled, his eyes brimming over with love. 'Hello, Ivy.'

The initial shock, followed by the wave of excitement

104

Ivy had felt as her eyes took in every detail, gave way to an overwhelming sense of relief, happiness and love, and in that moment, Ivy knew that she and Ned would make it through anything and everything life tossed in their path.

She smiled back and couldn't resist one tiny tease. 'Hello, Ned. I like what you've done with the place. Were you expecting someone else?'

Ned's eyes sparkled with devilment and he glanced at his watch. 'Yes, but not for fifteen minutes, so there's plenty of time. There's something I've been meaning to ask you for a while now.'

'Oh! And what might that be?'

He lifted the tip of his tie and waved it back and forth. 'Do you really like me in this tie? Because I have to tell you, it feels like I'm being throttled.'

Ivy grinned. 'You may well be, very soon. And yes, I do, but I prefer you out of it.'

'In that case...' He pressed a small remote which he must have been holding in his hand and her all-time favourite song, the one by Bryan Adams for the Kevin Costner film, *Robin Hood: Prince of Thieves* began playing in the background. This was her mum's favourite film and one that Ivy and Holly had sat and watched with Janet, time and time again until they loved it as much as she did.

'I love this song,' Ivy said, but I can never remember what it's called even though I know all the words.'

'I know you do. It's either called *Everything I Do*, or, *I Do It For You*. Or both. We'll check later, but for now...' He pulled a small, intricately carved wooden box from his jacket pocket and opened the lid. He got down on one knee and held the box out towards her. 'Ivy Gilroy, will you please put me out of my misery and once and for all, say you'll be my wife?'

105

Ivy burst out laughing and tears of joy began to fill her eyes. 'Not the most romantic proposal I've ever heard,' she said, sashaying towards him. 'But you did save my life once, so what the hell.'

'Save your life?' Ned smiled and got to his feet. 'I'd wear a tie for you!'

Ivy laughed again at the play on words of a line from the film but her laughter was replaced with amazement when she saw what the box contained: Two beautifully carved identical rings clearly made by Ned, but covered in gold, she assumed by Graham, a goldsmith who was a friend of Ned's. The carvings were a vine of Ivy wound around seven tiny horseshoes.

'Oh Ned! They're amazing.'

He took out the one made to fit her ring finger and slid it on. It was perfect, just as she knew it would be the moment she saw it. Ivy took the one made to fit Ned and slid it on his finger.

'I love you, Ned Stelling. Far more than you'll ever know, I think.'

'I love you, Ivy. I always have and I always shall.'

He leant forward to kiss her but she held him gently back with her hands. 'Did Holly or Mum, or maybe Gramps, tell you I was planning to propose to you tonight?'

Ned seemed genuinely surprised. 'You were planning to propose to me? No. Were you really?'

Ivy nodded. 'But it wasn't going to be anything as incredible as this. I feel almost ashamed now that I hadn't planned it better. I was just going to tell you how much I loved you, and give you a long speech I've written – which took me hours and hours, let me tell you.'

'No one said a word.' Ned shook his head. 'Damn I wish they had. I would've waited and let you do all the work. You have no idea how difficult it was to get all these red roses in here without Meg Stanbridge or anyone else noticing.'

'I prefer your proposal,' Ivy said. 'This is something we'll remember all our lives, and bore our kids senseless with by constantly retelling it.'

Ned nodded in agreement and smiled. 'So let's hear the speech.'

'Later,' Ivy said, undoing his tie. 'Let's get this tie off you before you choke to death. I can think of a much better use for it, as it happens. What's under those silver platters, by the way?'

Ned swept her up in his arms and carried her over to the cushions. 'I'll tell you later,' he said. 'Much, much later.'

Then he kissed her before she had a chance to say another word.

Chapter Sixteen

Rachel heard it the moment she woke up. It sounded like an army marching across the roof of Ivy Cottage, each individual wearing boots with several rows of nails in the soles. And they'd turned on a hose and aimed it at the windows while they were at it. She'd heard heavy rain before, and the rain on Friday night was like marbles bouncing on a drum, but this was unbelievable.

She dragged her arm from beneath the covers and glanced at her watch. Seven forty-five and a few seconds. Despite feeling like death warmed over, she threw off the duvet, slid her feet into her slippers and padded over to the window, tugging back the curtain to look out.

The sun would be rising about now, but the thick, charcoal grey clouds obscured all trace of it. All she could see was cloud and hail. Hail? Yep. That was definitely hail, and the hailstones were the size of golf balls. She watched several as they pounded into the muddy garden, sending tentacles of brown sludge up into the air. Poor Monty. She hoped he wasn't desperate for a pee. But then she remembered what Lucas had said on Saturday morning: about using a bucket and newspaper, and smiled. It may not be ideal but at least the poor dog wouldn't have to dodge incoming missiles.

She needed coffee, and she needed it right now. Pulling the curtain back to shut out the atrocious weather, she turned away and headed towards the stairs. What on earth was that? It sounded as if it had come from Mistletoe Cottage and the only thing that she could think of which was similar to the noise she had just heard, was the time when one of Sonia's ex-boyfriends had been so drunk that he'd fallen out of bed and onto the floor. He'd been like a solid, tree-sized log when he'd hit the bedroom carpet but amazingly, he'd stumbled away with only a bruise and nothing broken.

Had Lucas fallen out of bed? Or Monty fallen off it? Were they okay? Why hadn't she asked for Lucas' phone number? It was all very well him only being next door, but in this weather and with those hailstones, it would be like fending off an artillery bombardment. She could always ignore it and assume everything was fine.

Who was she kidding? She'd have to go and check. She marched back up the few stairs and went to get dressed. Coffee would have to wait. She pulled on her jeans and a jumper and hurried to the hall. Throwing her coat over her head like a shawl and grabbing her umbrella from the stand, she opened the front door and made a run for it.

Hailstones pelted down but the umbrella held them off and although her jeans were wet up to her knees by the time she reached the door of Mistletoe Cottage a few moments later, she was otherwise unaffected by what the weather had thrown at her.

The cottage was in darkness but she could hear Monty barking. Before ringing the bell, she took a peek through the letterbox and Monty, on hearing the flap lift up, came bounding down the hall to greet her. Then she heard Lucas' voice.

'Hello? Harry, is that you? The door's open. Please

109

come in. I may need a bit of a hand.'

'No, it's me,' Rachel said, opening the door and stepping into the hall, shaking the worst of the water from the umbrella as she did so. 'I heard a loud noise, like someone falling and I… oh Lucas!'

Lucas was sitting on the floor at the foot of the stairs. He was wearing nothing but a pair of boxer shorts and a cardigan, which was hanging half off his right shoulder. She dropped the umbrella, flicked on the hall light and dashed to his side, followed by Monty who then sat on the bottom stair and tried to lick his master's face. Lucas gently held him off with his hand.

'Good boy,' he said, patting Monty's head.

'Lucas, what happened? Are you all right?'

He greeted her with a smile but his face was ashen and when he tried to move his legs, he winced in pain.

'I think so. It was my own fault. I got up to get a drink of water and stupidly didn't turn on the lights. Monty was lying at the top of the stairs and I didn't see him. I'm not sure who was more surprised when I tripped over him. Me or Monty.'

At the mention of his name, Monty barked.

'Shush, boy,' Lucas said, petting him again.

Rachel glanced up the flight of stairs and felt sick.

'You fell all the way down?'

'I think I bounced, actually. One step at a time, from top to bottom.' He grinned, and winced again. 'I'm sure I'm fine but it's knocked the wind out of me and I can't seem to get to my feet at the moment.'

'Oh my God, Lucas. You may have broken something.' Her eyes scanned the length of him. Nothing looked twisted, and there was no sign of blood, but that wasn't necessarily a good thing.

He shook his head. 'I don't think so. I think I'll have a few bruises though. And now you're here, I've definitely got one to my pride. Sorry about this.'

She crouched down beside him and eased his back from against the wall, gently pulling his cardigan back onto his shoulder. He didn't indicate he was in pain when she did that, so at least his top half was okay... hopefully.

'Don't be ridiculous, Lucas,' she said, smiling at him. 'You've got nothing to be sorry for – apart from not turning on the lights, of course – and pride doesn't come into it. But we need to keep you warm. It's important after a shock I believe, or so my Auntie Elsie always says. Hot tea and blankets cures everything, according to her. Do you want to see if I can help you up? Or would you rather I got you a blanket and called the emergency services to check you haven't done any serious damage?'

He grinned at her. 'I'm fine. Honestly. But the tea does sound good, and if you don't mind me leaning on you, perhaps you'd help me into the kitchen.'

'I don't mind at all. But I think we should get you into the sitting room so that you can lie on the sofa. After that, I'll make some tea. But first, I think I should turn on some more lights. It's still a little dark in here.'

The early morning light was filtering along the hallway through the open front door, giving just enough light to see, but the sitting room curtains were still drawn, and the room was in complete darkness save for a chink on the threshold. She stood up and walked down the hall towards the living room, turning on the lights as she went along.

'Right. Are you ready?' she said, returning to Lucas' side.

'As ready as I'll ever be. We're a right pair, aren't we? You try to crack your head open and I attempt to break every bone in my body.'

'Hmm. And guess who instigated both actions.' She

111

gave Monty a reprimanding look but remorse surged through her when he whimpered and lowered his head. 'Oh, it's all right, Monty. I didn't mean it. They were accidents. It wasn't your fault.'

He raised his head and barked and when she met Lucas' eyes, she saw genuine warmth in them.

'Come on then,' she hastily added. 'Let's get you up. What do you want me to do?'

'. If you'll wrap your arms around me, I might be able to stand. Slip your right arm under mine and your left arm around my back and we'll give it a go, if you're happy to?'

'Oh Lucas, of course I'm happy to wrap my arms around you. Um... I mean.' She had *really got to stop* saying things like that out loud! She'd better try and make a joke of it. 'You didn't have to throw yourself down the stairs so that I would do so. You only had to ask.'

Something flashed across his eyes but was gone one second later.

'Damn,' he said, his eyes twinkling with amusement and his lips twitching with laughter. 'I should've known you'd see right through my cunning plan. The things a guy thinks he has to do to get attention around here.'

'Okay,' she said, doing exactly what he'd asked. Her arms were tingling and her heart was racing – and that was before she'd even tried to lift him. When he slid his right hand around her and squeezed her shoulder, she almost gasped. She coughed and attempted to regain her composure. 'One, two, three. Lift.'

Rachel had no idea how much Lucas weighed; he had an athletic-looking frame and was somewhere in the region of six foot tall, she imagined, but trying to get him off the floor was like trying to raise a sunken liner from the seabed. He was a deadweight. It was probably because of the way he was positioned and because he seemed reluctant to put too much weight on his ankles.

She heaved with all her might and suddenly, he was getting to his feet.

'Sorry. I thought I'd done something to my feet and I didn't want to put too much pressure on them. They were tingling at the first attempt but they're fine and...oh.' He wobbled slightly and Rachel took his weight to hold him firm. 'Er. I think I may have spoken too soon.'

'Have you broken your foot?' He seemed to be leaning to one side and his right foot was slightly raised.

He shook his head. 'I think it's my ankle. But it's probably just a slight sprain and it'll be fine once I've rested it. And once I've had that cup of tea, of course,' he joked.

She helped him limp to the sitting room sofa where he slowly lowered himself down.

'I'll get a blanket first, make some tea and after that, I'll light the wood burner. Are you okay?'

'Fine thanks. There's a throw over there.' He pointed to a tartan throw, neatly folded across the back of an armchair. 'It comes with the cottage.'

She got it and wrapped it around him – which was an oddly exciting experience. Images of getting on the sofa with him and snuggling up beneath the throw flashed like a slide show in her mind.

'You can't take advantage of an injured man.'

'Sorry, what?' Lucas was giving her a curious look.

Oh dear God, she'd done it again!

'Um. I said I should take care tucking a blanket over an injured man. I wouldn't want to make things worse.'

'Oh,' he said. 'Well, you're making this injured man feel a whole lot better, so no worries there.'

'I'll make the tea,' she said, and raced into the kitchen as if her life depended on it.

113

What on earth was the matter with her? She really had to get a grip.

Rachel made Lucas some sweet tea and ensuring he was comfortable, she fed Monty. Lucas told her how much food to put in Monty's bowl and Monty watched her intensely as if to make certain that she got it right. He gave a little bark of thanks and wolfed down the contents in a matter of seconds. To her relief, when he had finished, he returned to sit by Lucas' side.

Rachel piled kindling in the wood burner and lit it and only when that was done did she finally make coffee for herself.

'Would you like some breakfast? Or another cup of tea at least?'

Lucas smiled. 'I think I've been enough trouble this morning without asking you to make breakfast for me.'

'You didn't ask. I offered. Besides, I'm starving and I could murder some toast, if you have any bread, that is.'

'In the bread bin. There's butter and marmalade in the fridge. Please help yourself.'

'Want some?'

'If you're making it anyway, yes please.'

She went to the kitchen, slotted four slices of bread into the large toaster and glanced out of the window. She was surprised to see that the hailstones had stopped and had been replaced by a light, misty drizzle. She spotted Holly walking down the path from her cottage and dashed into the hall, grabbed her raincoat and raced outside.

'Holly. Sorry, but do you have a minute?'

Holly stopped and turned to face her, smiling at Rachel from beneath her umbrella.

'Good morning, Rachel. Of course I do. Is everything okay?'

Rachel saw the look on Holly's face and realised

what she must be thinking. It was still early, probably somewhere around eight, and Holly was no doubt wondering why Rachel was running down the path from the cottage where Lucas was staying, at that time in the morning.

'I heard a loud noise, like someone falling down the stairs,' she said, by way of explanation. 'I rushed round to check and found Lucas in a heap in the hall. I wondered if there is a doctor nearby.'

'Oh my God! Is he okay? Is he hurt? Shall I get Gabriel?'

'He says he's fine. I don't think any bones are broken and we managed to get him to the sofa, but he was limping and his ankle hurts. I thought it would be good to get a doctor to check. He won't go to the hospital though. He says there's no point in making a drama and that after a little rest, he'll be fine.'

Holly tutted. 'Typical man. I'll call Mum. Dr Barrett is a personal friend of hers. I'm sure she'd be happy to give him a call and ask him to pop round. Is there anything else you need?'

'No thanks. We're good.'

Holly rang Janet, told her what had happened, and just as Holly had said she would, Janet offered to call her doctor friend.

'Thanks, Mum,' Holly said. 'See you later.' She slipped her phone back in her bag and smiled at Rachel. 'She's going to call him, right now and ring me straight back. May I come and see Lucas?'

'Of course.'

'I was just making breakfast,' Rachel said as she and Holly reached Mistletoe Cottage. 'Would you like a cup of coffee or something?'

Holly shook her head. 'Not for me, thanks. Ooh, that must be Mum.' She retrieved her ringing phone from her bag and Rachel went into the kitchen while Holly made her way to the sitting room.

Rachel removed the toast, which was still warm thankfully and coated it with butter and marmalade. After making more tea and coffee, she placed everything on a tray and returned to the sitting room.

'I wondered where you'd run off to,' Lucas said, smiling at her. 'There was no need to find a doctor though. I told you I'm fine.'

'I know you did. But it's better to be safe than sorry.'

'Dr Barrett will be here around eight-thirty,' Holly said. 'If you're sure there's nothing I can do, Lucas, I'll leave you in Rachel's safe hands.' She smiled at Rachel. 'If that's okay with both of you, of course? I'll get Gabriel if you'd rather.'

'No need for that,' Lucas said. 'I'm perfectly happy in Rachel's hands, and anyway, I'm fine. There's no need for anyone to be here.'

'I'm staying,' Rachel said. 'At least until the doctor's been.'

'Great,' Holly said. 'I promised Ivy I'd meet her in The Coffee Hideaway. She was so excited when she called this morning to tell me what happened last night. You'll never believe this, Rachel, but she didn't get a chance to propose to Ned. He only went and proposed to her, didn't he? And apparently the smithy looked – to use Ivy's words – "like something out of one of Gabriel's romance novels". He'd even made matching Eternity rings for them both.'

'Wow!' Rachel said. 'I'm impressed. Please give her my congratulations. I hope she tells me all about it later.'

Holly laughed. 'I'm sure she will. I'm sure she'll be telling everyone. In fact, I don't suppose we'll be able to get her to shut up about it. I don't think I've ever heard her quite so happy. Apart from when she found out about

116

the babies, of course. She really was over the moon both then and this morning.'

'Say congratulations from me too, please,' Lucas said.

'Will do. I hope the doctor says everything's okay, Lucas. Please call me if you need anything. Gabriel's going to be in, working on his book, for most of the day, so don't hesitate to bang on the door if you want to. He won't mind at all. In fact, knowing him, he'll probably welcome the distraction. He says he's stuck on a particular chapter and it's driving him mad. Between you and me, I think it would do him good to get his mind off the book for a while.'

'Perhaps I could ask Gabriel to take Monty for a walk?' Lucas suggested. 'He'll need one before long.'

'That's an excellent idea,' Holly said. 'Bye then. See you later.'

'I could take Monty for a walk,' Rachel said, after saying goodbye to Holly.

'He's a bit of a handful.'

'What? And I'm some weak, pathetic woman? I'm stronger than I look. I lifted you off the floor for heaven's sake, and you're no lightweight, let me tell you.'

Lucas laughed. 'Thanks.'

'You're welcome. Seriously, Lucas, I can cope with Monty.'

Monty barked, got his feet and wagged his tail.

'You see,' she added. 'He even agrees with me.'

Lucas frowned. 'He knocked you flying in your kitchen.'

'Yes. But only because I wasn't expecting it. It'll be different when he's on his lead. Monty!' Rachel called his name and patted her hands against her legs. Monty raced towards her, jumped up and placed his paws on her

117

arms before trying to lick her face. 'You see. He comes when I call his name and I didn't even stumble when he jumped up. Good boy, Monty. Good boy.' She patted his head and rubbed his tummy.

'Okay. I'm convinced. If you're absolutely sure you don't mind.'

'I don't mind at all, Lucas. I think Monty and I are going to have some fun.'

'That's what I'm afraid of. When Monty starts having fun, mayhem usually isn't far behind. My ex-girlfriend can attest to that.'

That was the first time Lucas had mentioned his ex since Friday night and Rachel didn't like the peculiar feeling it had given her. Did he still have feelings for the girl? Did he want her back?

Chapter Seventeen

According to Dr Barrett, Lucas had thankfully only sustained a slight sprain to his right ankle and would be fine in a day or two, provided he rested and didn't do anything stupid.

'I think that means you're pretty much housebound for the next two days,' Rachel said. 'This holiday is turning into a bit of a nightmare, isn't it? What with the appalling weather and now this.'

'The doctor didn't say I had to stay indoors,' Lucas replied. He merely told me I had to rest and not do anything stupid. Well, I can rest just as easily in The Snowdrop Inn or The Coffee Hideaway or wherever else, as I can here. And I'll make sure I turn on all the lights in future. That about covers everything. As for this holiday turning into a nightmare, I'd say it was the exact opposite. It's already been one hundred times better than I thought it would be and it's only Monday.'

Rachel felt the same way about the holiday so far, but she didn't want to admit it to Lucas. She was definitely beginning to feel as if she was getting a bit of a crush on him and if he did still have feelings for his ex, that wasn't the best idea.

'Are you sure you didn't bump your head on the way

down those stairs. It's done nothing except rain since the moment we arrived. Although I suppose the hail this morning did add some variety.'

Lucas grinned. 'Admit it, Rachel. You're having as much fun as I am. Well, until I threw myself down a flight of stairs. I can't believe how friendly everyone is in this place. Gramps told me that people arrive here as strangers but leave here as friends. That's true, isn't it, don't you think?'

'Absolutely. The minute I met Holly and Gabriel, I felt as if I had made two new friends. And when I was doing Ivy's hair last night, it was as if I'd known her and Holly for years. I can't wait to hear all about Ned's proposal. I wonder if she'll be in the pub later.'

'We could go there for lunch if you like. You'll have to do the driving though, unfortunately. Or I could book a cab. There must be some around, even in a village as small as this. Eastbourne will definitely have some. Oh. Unless you have other plans, that is.'

'Nope. No plans at all. And I'm happy to drive. But are you really sure you should be going out?'

'Yes. It's only a little after nine so I can rest for three hours. I'm sure it'll be much better by half past twelve. Besides, I need to buy a walking stick or something to lean on, just for a day or two. You see, I'm taking the doctor's advice and being sensible. And I'd quite like to nip into Holly's bookshop, The Book Orchard. If I'm going to have to rest, I need some good books to read.'

'You can lean on me, Lucas. Oh! Um. I mean… you can use my arm for support from here to the car and suchlike. Or, when I take Monty for a walk in a minute, I can pop down to the village and get you a walking stick. And if you tell me the sort of books you like, I can get you those.'

His eyes sparkled and for a few seconds Lucas simply

120

gazed at her. Rachel could feel the flushing in her cheeks and the increased pace of her heart beat.

'Drew was mad to want to take a break from you,' he said, finally. 'If you were my girlfriend, I'd never want to let you go.'

She met his eyes and he suddenly looked as surprised as she was by what he had just said.

He laughed nervously and added: 'God that sounded a bit creepy. You'll probably start thinking I'm a serial killer again or something. Like you did on Friday night.'

'No, Lucas. I think we've both established that you're definitely not a serial killer. Monty on the other hand... Well, that's a different story. And speaking of Monty, I think it's about time I took him for a walk. He's probably bursting. Where is he, by the way? I haven't seen him since the doctor arrived.'

Lucas grinned. 'I think he thought the doctor was a vet and that he'd better get out of the way. My friend's a vet, and he sometimes makes house calls, providing there is pizza and beer afterwards. Monty's no doubt upstairs, hiding in his bed. I'm afraid you'll probably have to go up there and get him.'

Rachel walked into the hall and called Monty's name, but she didn't hear a murmur, a whimper, or bark in response.

'You're right. I'll have to go up there and get him.'

'Don't fall down,' Lucas called after her. 'This sofa's not big enough for both of us to lie on unless...' His voice trailed off as if he'd thought better of what he was going to say.

As she went upstairs to get Monty, she wondered if Lucas had read any of the kind of books Auntie Elsie had sent her. Like her, he seemed to be saying a lot of things out loud lately that he was probably wishing he hadn't.

121

Chapter Eighteen

The Book Orchard was about halfway up Market Street and virtually opposite Laurel French's café, The Coffee Hideaway. Both Rachel and Lucas had seen it when they went to the café for breakfast on Saturday. It was a pretty little shop with a forest green frontage and double doors between two, square bay windows. Inside, wooden shelves crammed full with books old and new, lined every wall. Comfy chairs and large, bean-filled cushions sat here and there and a warm, red rug covered original, polished oak floorboards. Customers could even bring their coffee from The Coffee Hideaway, and sit awhile. It was a book lover's dream. Rachel and Lucas agreed it was the kind of place they could each spend a morning or an afternoon without even noticing the passing of time.

So, despite Rachel's earlier offer to get Lucas some books, he'd asked her if she'd mind if they popped in for a browse, after lunch. Fortunately, he had taken her up on her offer to find him a walking stick, which meant that, other than using the stick, Lucas could walk unaided. And that meant Rachel could hold Monty's lead and still have one hand free.

'Are dogs allowed?' Rachel asked Holly, popping her head around one of the double doors but ensuring Monty stayed outside.

'As long as they're well-behaved,' Holly replied, with a smile.

Lucas looked down at Monty and grinned. 'That means you'll have to stay out here then.'

Monty barked softly, pushed past Rachel and sat down inside, directly in front of the door.

'Well, that told you!' Holly laughed. 'How's the ankle? When Rachel came looking for a walking stick, she popped in and told me the diagnosis.'

'It's feeling better already. I've been resting it all morning. It's good to get out though.'

'He's not a very patient, patient,' Rachel added. 'He doesn't enjoy being confined to the sofa.'

'Well, not on my own,' Lucas said.

'When Monty and I got back after our walk, Lucas behaved as if we'd been gone for days.'

Holly laughed but Lucas frowned.

'It felt as if you had. That is… I'm not used to anyone else taking Monty for a walk.'

'Did you start to think something may have happened to us?' Rachel teased.

'You have no idea what went through my mind while you were gone.' He gave a little cough. 'This place is incredible, Holly. Gabriel told me it's only been open a few months, but when you look around it gives the impression that it's been here for years and years.'

'The shop itself has,' Holly said. 'We decided to keep the forest green frontage, which amazingly came up beautifully after a thorough clean. The shelves were here and we painted them to match the outside. The floorboards merely needed cleaning and polishing. Mum had the rug rolled up in one of the attic rooms of The Snowdrop Inn and although I could've purchased a new one, this one is perfect and adds to the antiquated feel.

But we also wanted a touch of modernity, so the cushions and chairs are brand new.'

'I love that big chair with the back shaped like an open book.'

Holly beamed at her. 'Gabriel had that custom-made. It's a love seat, so two people can sit on it, if they're friends or are happy to snuggle up. The cushions with the photos of the shop front, were made by a friend of Ivy's. Obviously, all the iron work lamp stands and bases were made by Ned.' She suddenly looked apologetic. 'Sorry. You didn't come in to hear about the shop. You came for books.'

'Don't apologise,' Rachel and Lucas said.

'I think it's fascinating,' Rachel added, with a smile.

'I expect this building could tell some tales,' Lucas said.

'It was empty when I got it, and had been for a long time, but prior to that it was once a sex shop for a short time.'

Rachel laughed. 'I bet that went down well with some of the locals.'

Holly grinned. 'I was just about to dash across to Laurel's and bring back a coffee and cake. Can I get some for you?'

'We haven't long ago had lunch,' Lucas said, 'but I for one can always make room for coffee and a cake. So yes please. Let me pay though.'

'No. My treat. Rachel?'

Rachel glanced towards the window and across the road to The Coffee Hideaway. 'Well, I think we may be here for some time, so coffee and cake sounds perfect. Thank you so much, Holly.'

'Would you like anything special? Gabriel always pops in for tea and cake around three, and Gramps is dropping by with Sarah, so I'll be getting a selection.'

'Anything's fine with me, thanks,' Lucas said.

'Same here,' agreed Rachel.

'Then I'll be back in a tick. Make yourselves at home. I'll ask Laurel for a bowl so that Monty can have some water. I'd hate him to feel completely left out.'

Monty barked, moved away from the door and settled down beside the book-shaped love seat.

'I think I'd like to move to Hideaway Down,' Lucas said, as Holly left the shop and crossed the road.

'Me too. We should move here together. Oh. I didn't mean... Um. What I meant was, we should both move here. Separately, of course.'

Lucas didn't say a word but as Rachel turned her back to hide the riot of red rushing across her cheeks, she could feel him watching her. She couldn't make up her mind whether she liked it or not, but only because she had no idea what he was thinking. If it was something along the lines of: "Forget it, honey. I'd sooner spend the rest of my life alone with Monty than consider moving in with you." That, she wouldn't like. Although technically, would he be living alone if he were living with Monty? Possibly not.

If, however, Lucas was watching her and thinking something like: "My darling Rachel. Nothing would make me happier than the thought of spending the rest of my life with you... and Monty of course." Well that, she *would* rather like.

As there was no way of knowing what the man was thinking, she couldn't decide whether she liked him watching her or not.

But on the whole, she was leaning towards the positive.

Chapter Nineteen

Life was pretty good for Janet Gilroy. Better than it had been for many, many years. Both her daughters were thriving, happy and in loving relationships. If you'd asked her that, this time last year, she would have said she was beginning to despair whether anyone in the Gilroy family would ever find love again. Now, Ivy was marrying Ned and expecting twins next year. Holly and Gabriel were also madly in love, and were probably heading in the same direction. Even her own father, Gordon Gilroy, was talking of marrying again. Sarah Saltcote might not been Janet's first choice for Gramps, but without doubt, Sarah made him happy and Janet would welcome with open arms, any woman whom Gordon said he loved. And he had said that he loved Sarah. The woman had a peculiar penchant for garden gnomes, which Janet, and even Gramps come to that, would never understand, but everyone had their faults and little foibles.

Suddenly, Janet was seriously starting to believe that the £15 she had handed over to Skylar Lake on the day of Petunia and Bartram's August wedding, may not have been a waste of money, after all.

Janet had never truly believed that there were people

who could predict another person's future, but when Harry Goode and Beatrix Wellesley, both of whom she'd known since they were born, came into The Snowdrop Inn after having their futures told by Skylar, she was prepared to be convinced. She decided then and there that £15 wasn't much to pay to be told what Fate had in store.

And as she told her good friend, Trixie French, whom she persuaded to go with her on that bright and sunny August day: 'If we don't like what this Skylar Lake tells us, we can just ignore it. We'll only believe it if she tells us something good.'

Trixie thought that was a very good plan. Especially when Skylar told Trixie that there would soon be a wedding in her family and that the prospective son-in-law had a very particular, if somewhat strange, connection with a vampire.

That could only mean one thing. Laurel French and Jamie McDay would soon be getting married. Although Trixie had sworn Janet to secrecy.

'You know what my darling Laurel's like,' Trixie said. 'The minute I tell her I know she'll be marrying Jamie, is the minute she'll tell me I'm wrong.'

As was often the case, Janet didn't agree with Trixie on that point, but she didn't say so. Nothing would stop Laurel from marrying Jamie, not even the fact that it was exactly what her mother wanted. Besides, since Jamie's arrival in Hideaway Down, the relationship between Trixie and Laurel had improved in leaps and bounds. So much so, that Janet thought Laurel might actually be prepared to listen to her mum's instructions. Well, some of them at least.

But Janet wasn't really thinking about what Skylar Lake had told anyone else. Not today. Not on this cold, grey, wet and windy Tuesday as she sat in her bedroom overlooking the pond and a sodden Market Field.

She remembered last Christmas when the field and the pond froze over and they held a Frost Fair-cum-Christmas market, and skated on the pond. When Holly met Gabriel and fell in love, and Ivy and Ned began their whirlwind relationship after being friends since they could walk. So much had changed since this time last year. And if Skylar Lake was to be believed, there were still several changes ahead.

So far, all that Skylar told her had come true and she had of course, been spot on with regard to Janet's past. Skylar knew about Janet's husband running off and their subsequent divorce, but that was common knowledge and perhaps Skylar had heard that somewhere. She knew Holly's previous heartbreak and of Ivy's recent accident. But it was when Skylar talked of the future that Janet's interest had been piqued.

Skylar had said that by November, Janet would be knitting baby clothes. A matching set of two. It was now the end of October so she'd better get started on that. That she would be paying for a Christmas wedding. Ned had proposed to Ivy and although they hadn't set a date, they both love Christmas and so it made sense.

Skylar said that someone called Grandpa or Grump or something similar would be moving to a house surrounded by little men with fishing rods. Janet couldn't expect Skylar to get Gramps' name precisely right, and most of Sarah Saltcote's gnomes held fishing rods.

She'd said that Janet would struggle with building works and that when she thought all hope was lost, someone with the initial 'B' would come into her life and solve all her problems. And he wouldn't simply be refurbishing her property, he would also help to rebuild her faith in men and mend her broken heart. The moment Billy Brookes had walked into The Snowdrop Inn and smiled at her, Janet somehow knew the man was here to stay – and that was before she knew his name. Gramps had been the one who'd taken Billy's booking and he had written William Rooks in the reservations book for the cottages. She and Billy had laughed about it on Saturday night when he had asked why the payment confirmation he had received had been made out to Mr William Rooks. Gramps really needed to have his hearing checked. She must arrange that for him. No, she would get Sarah to arrange it.

She wondered how Holly and Ivy would feel if Billy and she became an item. They'd want her to be happy, she had no doubt of that. But would they want her to marry again? Did *she* want to marry again? Why was she even thinking about marriage? She'd only met the guy four days ago? But as she always said: 'Anything can happen in Hideaway Down.'

If Skylar Lake was genuine and really could predict the future, there'd be more than one wedding in The Snowdrop Inn between now and this time next year.

There was only one blip on Janet's otherwise exceptionally sunny horizon – not taking into account today's appalling weather, of course.

Skylar Lake had also predicted a storm. A storm that would come from nowhere and would cause a lot of damage. A storm that, if Janet made the wrong decision, would also take a life.

No matter how many times Janet asked, and in spite of offering to pay whatever it took, Skylar Lake had been unable to see whose life it was, or what the outcome would be, and had refused to take more than the £15 she had already taken.

Janet, being Janet, had pushed this one dark cloud to the deepest recesses of her mind. But as the things Skylar Lake had predicted, were one by one coming true, the larger and more threatening this dark cloud was becoming.

The storm on Friday had been bad which was why she had told everyone to gather at The Snowdrop Inn. Apart from the tree falling across the road, no one had been hurt, let alone lost their life and Janet wondered whether her actions had sent that cloud away. But something was still telling her to be ready. To be prepared. And despite her laughter and her jokes and her willingness to look on the bright side of life whenever she possibly could, she was feeling anxious.

Janet was a woman who never prayed, but she wondered if she should start. Just once or twice. She was going to church today. That would take everyone by surprise. Perhaps the Reverend Kevin Longbourne would drop down dead with astonishment. She sincerely hoped not and realised she shouldn't joke about such things.

Kev-the-Rev often joked that Janet Gilroy would only come to church for anything other than christenings, weddings or funerals if one of the four horsemen of the apocalypse picked her up and threw her over his saddle.

But Janet valued Kevin's opinion and she had to discuss this niggling doubt with someone other than Trixie French. Trixie may be her lifelong best friend, but sensible, practical advice was not something Trixie was known for. Kevin Longbourne, on the other hand, most definitely was. And if the weather this week continued as it had, another storm couldn't be far off the horizon. Although the weathermen weren't predicting one. Which was exactly what Skylar Lake had said. Janet Gilroy may not know what she should do, but she hoped Kevin Longbourne would.

Chapter Twenty

Rachel couldn't believe it was Tuesday already. She would be leaving on Friday, which meant that today was halfway through the week. The days seemed to be flying. She thought that she would be wishing the days away. Instead, she wished that she could slow down time. Or that she could stay in Hideaway Down for longer.

Yesterday had been a special day. She had really enjoyed taking care of Lucas and loved taking Monty for his walk in the morning. Lunch with Lucas and Monty in the pub, followed by a long, leisurely afternoon in Holly's bookshop had made it the perfect day.

Even Beatrix Welsley turning up at The Book Orchard, making Lucas go all 'fan-boy' hadn't diminished Rachel's pleasure. Beatrix was lovely and Rachel liked her very much. But then, Rachel liked everyone she had met in Hideaway Down. Particularly Lucas Webb.

The evening had been spent in The Snowdrop Inn and she could understand completely why the place was so popular. It had found a special place in her heart and she was only here on holiday. Billy Brookes had said that the place felt like an old pair of slippers. That made Janet scowl at him until he explained.

'It's like coming home after a hard day at work,' he said, 'and taking off your heavy boots and wiggling your toes in the warmth and comfort of your favourite slippers.'

Rachel knew what he meant. Working on her feet all day nothing felt as good as getting home, kicking off her shoes and putting on her fluffy, cosy penguin-character ones. Janet must have understood that too because she smiled at him and gave him a pint 'on the house'.

When Rachel and Lucas had driven back to the cottages, Rachel offered to help Lucas in. Then Gabriel and Holly came home and Gabriel insisted on helping instead. Holly throwing him irritated looks hadn't made Gabriel realise that he might be 'stepping on Rachel's toes'. Rachel said goodnight and went back to Ivy Cottage, taking one of the Gabriella Mann books she'd bought that day, to bed. It was clearly the only romance she'd be getting but she still went upstairs with a smile.

And today was a new day, full of hope and promise. Rachel leapt out of bed and threw back the curtains. It was also a day full of rain. Nothing new there then. She wouldn't let the weather get her down. It had rained virtually nonstop since she arrived but in spite of that, she'd had fun. Or possibly because of it.

The power wouldn't have failed if it hadn't been for the storm. Lucas wouldn't have turned up at her back door. They wouldn't have spent the evening together enjoying a candlelit dinner and wine, and they wouldn't have gone to The Snowdrop Inn with Holly and Gabriel and met all the villagers.

She and Lucas would have still met, no doubt. And Holly and Gabriel would still have invited them to the pub. But would they have had the banter and easy-going friendship they seemed to have developed if it hadn't been for a storm, a power failure, some chilli, rice and wine, and a few little candles?

That was one of the vagaries of life. Change one of those things and she and Lucas could be spending a completely different holiday right now, each doing their own thing separately from one another.

But they weren't. And Monty would be waiting to go for a walk and Lucas would be waiting for his breakfast. Or perhaps trying to make it himself even though she had insisted in the pub last night that she would make him breakfast and walk Monty. Lucas had said he was sure his ankle would be better in the morning but she'd be more than welcome to join him for breakfast, if she wanted to.

She showered and dressed, wondering why she hadn't brought anything with her other than jeans and jumpers and one pair of smart, black trousers. Perhaps she could pop into Eastbourne later and buy something. A pretty dress maybe? And a pair of leather knee-high boots would keep off the rain and mud just as well as any of her walking boots. They would also look far more feminine and sexy.

She could ask if Ivy would like to join her on a little shopping spree. Or she could go alone. That would be just as much fun. Gabriel had asked Lucas if he would tell him a couple of things about Lucas' design process to help Gabriel get inside his architect-hero's head, so Lucas would be happily occupied this morning. She could go to Eastbourne after taking Monty for his walk.

Having decided on her plans, she grabbed her raincoat and stepped out into the rain. She was definitely ready for breakfast. Her tummy was rumbling like the thunder she could hear way off in the distance. There was another storm coming but she smiled. Not even the prospect of another storm could dampen her spirits. In fact, she was rather looking forward to it. Especially if she was with Lucas and the power went out again.

Chapter Twenty-One

'Where have you two been?' Janet asked, as Rachel approached the bar of The Snowdrop Inn that evening. 'I haven't seen you all day. You're looking very pretty. New dress?'

'Is it that obvious? When Lucas said I looked lovely, I pretended it was one I'd had for ages. I don't know why I did that.'

Janet smiled. 'We all do that. Lucas will never know. Men never do. It's only because you were fiddling with the top as you walked over here that I thought it was probably new.'

Rachel pulled a face. 'I bought it in Eastbourne this morning. I went on a little shopping spree. The top didn't look quite this low cut or this tightly fitted when I tried it on in the shop. I'm terrified my boobs will fall out. Or that everyone will think I look like a tart.'

'You don't look anything like a tart but you do look sexy. And the top's not as low cut as you probably think it is. Your boobs are safe, believe me.'

'Phew. That's a relief. Thanks. Sexy was what I was going for. The boots are new too, and I did admit that to Lucas. Well, he knew I was going to Eastbourne, so I had to come back with something. I just didn't want him to think I'd bought a whole new wardrobe just for him.'

Janet grinned. 'Even though you have.'

Rachel nodded. 'Not just for him though. It's been ages since I bought any new clothes and certainly nothing as sexy as this. I just wanted to feel…'

'Good?'

'Yes. And now that I know the menfolk won't be getting an eyeful of my boobs, I do feel good.'

'Did you buy anything else?'

'Another dress, a really pretty blouse and a pleated skirt.'

'Gosh. You really did go to town. Well done you. A pint for Lucas and your usual, is it?'

'Yes please. It's very strange because I don't often wear skirts or dresses. Unless I'm going out somewhere. Most of the time I live in jeans or trousers. That's what I was going to buy. Trousers. But this dress sort of… called to me. Then the other one did. And so did the skirt.'

'Ah yes,' Janet said, smiling. 'The siren song of shopping. It's a call we women can't resist. And why should we? We're worth it, after all.'

'You're right. We are. When Drew… dumped me, and let's be honest, he did that pretty spectacularly even if he didn't have the guts to tell me, I felt very… unworthy. I thought I clearly wasn't good enough to keep him interested. I thought I needed to… improve. My Auntie Elsie even sent me some of those self-help slash self-improvement books.'

'Oh God. Don't get me started on those. Did they help?'

'Not sure. I talk to myself a lot more these days. Out loud, too. Usually when I really shouldn't. But other than that the one thing they did say, and I do agree with, is that we should all strive to be the best 'us' that we can be. I don't think it was those exact words, but you get what I mean.'

'I do. Or as Gramps would say: "Be true to yourself and do your best." I think that's good advice. We shouldn't try to mould ourselves into someone we're not.' She glanced up and grinned, nodding towards the door. 'I think I could do with going on a little shopping spree myself, to bring out the best of me. There's someone I'd quite like to look sexy for.'

Rachel turned and saw Billy Brookes smiling in their direction. It was clear he only had eyes for Janet.

'From the look he's giving you, Janet, I think you already do.' Rachel paid for the drinks and Janet winked at her. 'I'll get out of the way. Have fun.'

'You too.'

Rachel turned to walk away and as she did so, she noticed that Lucas was looking directly at her. Forget about her boobs falling out of her dress, her heart was about to burst in her chest. Unless she was very much mistaken, Lucas Webb had exactly the same look in his eyes as Billy Brookes. And that could only mean one thing.

Chapter Twenty-Two

'I still can't get used to how dark it is here,' Lucas said, getting out of Rachel's car. 'I'm not sure whether I'll be glad to be able to get back from the pub when I'm back in Oxford and not have to use a torch to see my way to the front door, or if I'll miss the total darkness of this place.'

'I'll definitely miss this place,' Rachel said. 'London will seem blinding after here.'

Lucas leant on his stick and slowly walked towards the door of Mistletoe Cottage. He could walk much faster but he didn't want to. His ankle still hurt but not enough to trouble him. He'd take things easy though, just in case. He didn't want to cause more damage to it.

That wasn't the reason he was proceeding at a snail's pace though. He had something on his mind and he needed time to think.

'It's ages since I've been to London,' he said. 'Perhaps I should think about spending a day there sometime soon. Or possibly a weekend. If I do, and you're free, maybe we could meet up. You know? For coffee or something. Or a drink. Maybe… dinner.'

'Um. That would be nice.'

She didn't sound exactly ecstatic about his suggestion

and Lucas was thankful she couldn't see his face. Perhaps he had entirely misjudged the situation. He had formed the impression that she liked him. Maybe he was wrong.

'I expect you've got a pretty hectic social life.'

'No. Not really.'

Christ, this was like pulling teeth. He had actually considered making a move tonight – taking her hand, or slipping an arm around her waist. He was going to invite her in, make her coffee – although she would probably insist on making it – turn the conversation towards more personal stuff. Boyfriend, girlfriend stuff. He had planned to ask about Drew. Find out if she still had feelings for the guy. If she wanted him back. No point in trying to start something if Rachel really wanted to be with someone else.

He'd even thought about finding a way to get her to sit next to him on the sofa. He'd move closer, lean in for a kiss, pull her into his arms.

Should he do it? Should he take the risk? It could ruin everything. They were comfortable together. They had fun. They talked. They laughed. They played with Monty. They had even read a book together. Well, they'd started to. He'd like them to finish it. But if he tried something and it turned out Rachel wasn't interested, all of that would go out the window. She might not want to see him again. Might avoid him for the rest of the week.

But boy did she look good. Especially tonight. She had looked good the moment he first laid eyes on her and she was one of those women who look really sexy in casual clothes like the jeans and jumpers he had seen her in all week so far. But tonight in that dress and those boots, he could hardly take his eyes off her. It had almost driven him nuts. And why did she have to keep putting her hand on her cleavage as if she was trying to hide the

139

hint of the enticing curves beneath. Her dress was low cut, but not enough to reveal anything. Each time her hand went up, all he could think about was moving it away with his and exploring every inch of her. He was sure she must have noticed.

Perhaps she had. Perhaps that was why, since the moment they had left the pub and got into her car, she had seemed distant. As if she was wondering how quickly she could get away from him tonight.

Even Monty seemed subdued. As if he could read Lucas' mind, and sensed trouble.

Perhaps it was better if he didn't try anything tonight. Didn't tell her how he felt. Didn't pull her into his arms and kiss her. Perhaps it was best to take things slowly and see how this developed. To see if he could do anything to get Rachel to like him even half as much as he liked her.

It was only Tuesday, after all. He had three more days to see how Rachel felt. And two more nights to kiss her.

Chapter Twenty-Three

'It's really weird, Sonia,' Rachel said, holding the phone to her ear the following morning. 'But since I've been here I haven't missed Drew at all. Apart from the first night, maybe. But even then, I don't think I was actually missing *him*, as much as missing the feeling of being part of a couple.'

'You obviously did the right thing by going on this holiday. Perhaps it was meant to be.'

Rachel smiled into the phone and studied her reflection in the dressing table mirror. She looked a lot more relaxed than she had a few days earlier. And happier. She felt it too. Relaxed, happy and oddly enough, actually looking forward to the future, whatever it might bring.

Although she had been disappointed last night. She had seen the way Lucas had been looking at her in the pub and her body was alive with the electricity of anticipation. From the moment they left the pub, all she could think about was the fact that he might finally kiss her.

He'd even mentioned the possibility of coming down to London. For once, she hadn't said exactly what was on her mind. 'Please come. You can stay with me. Spend the weekend. Although you won't see much of London if you do. You won't see more than my bedroom.' But thankfully she hadn't said that. She couldn't even remember what she had said. He hadn't taken it further, so it was probably just a throwaway line. Just something friends would say to one another.

That's all they really were. Friends. That was abundantly clear after last night. He might have thought she look sexy, but not sexy enough to want to do anything about it. Not sexy enough for him. Perhaps she simply wasn't his type of woman. Not the type he'd want to take to bed at least.

But did that really matter? They got on extremely well. They were comfortable in each other's company. They were friends. If nothing else came of it, at least she would have had a brilliant holiday. A really good time. It actually was possible to go away on your own and have fun. Who knew?

'Perhaps it was, Sonia,' she said, sighing into the phone. Mum always says that things happen for a reason. Oh, that's the doorbell.'

'Lu-c-as,' Sonia teased, stretching out his name and raising her voice in a sing-song fashion at the end. 'Where are you and he off to now?'

'I'm not sure.' Rachel walked into the hallway and trotted down the stairs. 'I wasn't expecting him until later. Ned invited him to the smithy today. Lucas wants to see Ned's work because Ned designs most of his own stuff and Lucas, as an architect, is really interested in all forms of art and design. Plus he wants some pieces of ironwork for a building he's working on, so he may commission Ned to make them. He seems very keen and from the stuff I've seen of Ned's, the man's a genius. A true master of his craft. Gabriel was driving him down there. At least, he said he would last night. Perhaps something's happened and he can't. Perhaps Lucas needs a lift.'

'Well, he can't keep away from you, whatever excuse he makes. Perhaps he's going to ask if you want to go with him. Is this just a holiday fling, Rachel?' Sonia's voice took on a serious tone. 'Or are you hoping it's going to go somewhere?'

Rachel stopped at the foot of the stairs. 'Oh. Um. I've no idea. I haven't thought that far ahead. I mean, nothing's actually happened between us, as far as romance goes. We're simply friends at the moment. But, yeah, I think I would like to see him again after we leave here. I'm not rushing into anything though, so don't worry. I think I need some time after what happened with Drew, and Lucas has just come out of a relationship himself, so we both want to take things slowly'

'That's remarkably sensible of you. And best not to get your hopes up, just in case. I don't want you to get hurt again so soon after Drew.'

'I won't. Although what's the point of living if we don't take a few risks now and then.'

The doorbell rang again, this time with more persistence.

'How very philosophical. Where in those bloody awful books did it say that?'

Rachel laughed and headed towards the front door. 'It didn't. Ivy said it in The Snowdrop Inn the other night. She was going to propose to her boyfriend – that's Ned by the way. Did I mention that? Anyway, he beat her to it and proposed in the most romantic way. I'll tell you all about it next time we chat. And she wouldn't have been taking a risk really because everyone knew he would say yes. Even me. Gotta go. Call you later. Have fun.'

'Can't wait to hear all about it. You have fun, too.'

Rachel pressed end call and yanked the front door

143

open, with a huge, happy smile on her face.

'Drew!' She couldn't believe her eyes. 'Wh-what are you doing here?'

'Getting bloody soaked at the moment. Can I come in?'

Without thinking, Rachel stepped aside to let him in.

'This place is the back end of beyond,' Drew said, shrugging off his saturated jacket, which clearly wasn't weatherproof. 'It's taken me a bloody lifetime to get here and I had to stop and ask directions three times. No wonder it's called Hideaway... whatever it is. That was part of the problem. I couldn't remember the sodding name your mum told me and she's not answering her phone.'

'You've spoken to Mum?'

'Yes. I went to the salon this afternoon.'

'And Mum told you where I was?'

'Yes.'

'Why?'

He gave her a look as if he thought she were demented or something. 'Because I asked her. What's up with you, Rach?'

'What's up with me! I'm in a state of shock, Drew, that's what's up with me. And what I meant was, why did you go to the salon?'

'Why? To find out where you were, of course. I've got a couple of days off.'

Rachel could feel her lower lip dropping and she snapped both lips together. He was behaving as if nothing had happened. As if they were still the best of friends, if not lovers. Why had he gone to ask her mum where she was? And why hadn't her mum called her to tell her that he had? But more importantly, why was he here?

'There's something wrong with your phone,' he

continued as he glanced around and, obviously spotting the coat hooks, hung up his sodden jacket, which immediately began to drip water into the umbrella stand and drip-tray below.

It was only then that she saw Drew's holdall on the floor. She hadn't noticed it when she'd opened the door and let him in, or even when he must have put it down to remove his jacket. But she was so astonished to see him that she hadn't taken in anything other than the fact that Andrew Walton was standing in front of her, his handsome face as gorgeous as ever and his smile just as sexy. That said, his immaculately combed hair wasn't quite as perfect as it usually was, no doubt due to the horrendous weather.

'My phone?' Rachel still couldn't get her head around what was happening.

'Yeah. I've been trying to call you since yesterday but it just goes to voicemail and you haven't called me back. I've tried to send messages but they're not going through. I don't get the 'delivered' sign on my phone. You need to deal with that or you'll keep missing important calls and texts.'

'Have you?' Rachel suddenly remembered that, the evening after she had gone to Drew's office where Jenny had dropped the bombshell, she and Sonia had opened a bottle of wine, got a bit tipsy and in an act of defiance and independence, had blocked Drew's number from her phone. No texts would get through and all calls would go straight to a special 'blocked numbers' inbox. But as she hadn't checked her voicemail for days, she hadn't seen any calls – which possibly also explained why she hadn't heard from her mum about his visit. There was probably a voicemail message that Rachel hadn't picked up.

'I just told you I have. Have you been drinking, Rach? You know how you get after a couple of glasses of wine.' He shook his head in a gesture of reprimand and pointed to the door to his right. 'Is that the sitting room? Is there a fire? I'm sodding freezing. Make me a cup of coffee would you, angel? Unless there's any whisky in this place, in which case, make it a large glass.'

'Drew!' Rachel pulled herself together. 'There isn't any whisky and I'm not making you anything until you tell me why you're here.'

Drew stopped in the doorway and turned to face her. 'Why are you so upset? I thought you'd be pleased to see me. I told you, Rach, I've got a couple of days off. I remembered you said you'd booked a cottage for us to have a romantic getaway and when I bumped into Sonia and she told me—'

'You've talked to Sonia? When? What did she say?'

He took a step towards her and reached out his hand. 'It doesn't matter what she said, Rach. What matters is I'm here.'

Rachel stepped back. 'No Drew. What matters is *why* you're here? The last time we spoke, you said that we should "take a break" and that we'd discuss it later. We never did. Because you wouldn't return any of *my* calls or *my* messages.'

He shrugged and frowned, coughing lightly as he ran a hand through his wet hair.

'Yeah. About that. You know what I'm like, Rach. You know I hate making decisions and I can't stand confrontations or unpleasant situations. I thought we should both take a little time out to think things through. I suppose I should've spoken to you when I got back from Edinburgh, but things got crazy at the office and I just didn't get a chance. But I'm here now. We've had our little break from each other, and now we can spend a couple of days together, working things out. Why are you looking at me like that? I suppose I can understand that you're a bit cross but you look as if you'd like to kill me right now. That's overdoing it a bit, don't you think?'

'Overdoing it? Think things through? Work things out? Did I really just hear you say all that? You waltz in here as if nothing's happened and expect me to welcome you with open arms? Is that really what you're saying? That you want me back? Aren't you forgetting something, Andrew bloody Walton?'

'Hey, Rach! There's no need to get stroppy. Okay, you're cross. Fair enough. Let's talk about it like civilised people. Please don't start ranting and raving.'

'Ranting and... You're unbelievable, Drew. Absolutely bloody unbelievable. Have you discussed this with Jenny? Or are you now taking a break from that relationship, too? What about the baby? Do you actually care about anyone other than yourself?'

Drew looked gobsmacked.

'Well? Say something!' Rachel crossed her arms and waited, taking deep breaths in the hope they would calm her. They didn't.

Drew glowered at her. 'If I knew what the bloody hell you were talking about, I might. What's my relationship with Jenny got to do with anything and why would I be "taking a break" from her, for Christ's sake? She's been with me since I started at Morcross James and she's the best secretary anyone could wish for. In fact, I'm pretty bloody annoyed she's gone and got herself up the duff. But she assures me that she'll only be off for two weeks or so and the minute she's able to, she'll be back at her desk, thank God. I don't think I could deal with all the hassle of replacing her – although I wouldn't tell her that, of course. No one's completely indispensable in the finance industry and I don't want her to start asking for a rise or something stupid. She'll probably want to do flexi-time as it is with a kid to take care of, and HR will probably insist I let her, even though it'll be sodding inconvenient.'

'Can you hear yourself?' Rachel was at boiling point. How could he be saying such things? How could she have been in love with a man who didn't give a damn about anyone else? 'My God, I almost feel sorry for Jenny. I couldn't believe it when she told me about your affair, although I'm not sure whether she told me about you and her, for my benefit or for hers, but it seems as if I don't know you at all. You're talking about her – and the baby – as if neither of them matter in the least to you. Except how it might affect your day at the office! This is the mother of your child, Drew. And *your* baby! Don't you care about them at all?'

'What? What affair? Are you telling me that you spoke to Jenny and that she said we were having an affair?'

'Yes. And don't try to pretend that you weren't. Or act all shocked like that. I came to your office when you wouldn't answer my calls. She told me to leave the two of you alone and that it was over between you and me. When I saw her stomach, I realised just how true that was.'

The colour drained from Drew's face and he shook his head so slowly that Rachel could virtually see the cogs turning over in his mind, as if he were trying to think of just the right thing to say to defend his actions. Not that he could say anything to achieve that. He had – and was – behaving appallingly.

'You think the baby's mine?' Drew squeaked, like a terrified little mouse, frozen in fear in front of a huge cat. 'Did… did Jenny actually *tell* you that it was?'

'Yes!' Rachel recalled that day in minute detail. 'Actually… no, not in those exact words. But then people rarely say exactly what they mean, do they? You said we should "take a break" when what you really meant was that you'd been cheating, you'd got your secretary pregnant and you and I were over. Albeit, several months after you should've told me you were seeing someone else. You told me you'd never cheat on anyone, Drew. But you cheated on me and now you want to cheat on Jenny. You're... you're a bastard, Andrew Walton. And I've got nothing more to say to you. You can let yourself out.'

She stormed towards the kitchen but a moment later, Drew was beside her in the narrow hall. He grabbed her arms and twisted her round to face him. His expression was one of fury, his face was red with anger, and turning a deeper red with each passing second.

'For your information, Rachel, I never *have* cheated on anyone. Not you. And certainly not Jenny − because there is no relationship between me and Jenny and there never, ever has been. Apart from that of boss and secretary, which I always thought was a good one... until now. I see I was wrong about that. I knew she liked me and she did come on a bit strong at one of the office Christmas parties, but I have no idea why she would pretend we were having an affair. I haven't slept with her so there is absolutely zero chance of that kid being mine. And I know for a fact it isn't. Because the father is her best friend's brother, who she told me herself, she stupidly had a fling with, even though she was in love with someone else.' He suddenly looked horrified. 'Bloody hell! I suppose I must be the *someone else.* Which is really sodding annoying, because now I *will* have to get another secretary. Bugger!'

149

Chapter Twenty-Four

'Lordy, Lordy me. Have you heard the news?' Meg Stanbridge burst into The Snowdrop Inn and waddled towards the bar.

'Hello, Meg,' Janet said. 'Usual, is it?'

Meg placed a chubby hand on her chest then struggled onto the stool nearest to where Janet stood on the other side of the bar.

'Janet Gilroy, you're a lifesaver. Yes please. I've said it before and I'll say it again. Your generosity knows no end.'

Janet grinned. As usual Meg had taken it for granted that she wouldn't have to pay for her rum and black. But then she never did pay for her drinks, so that was understandable.

'What's the news then, Meg?' Janet poured Meg her drink and place it on the bar in front of her.

'Well, I haven't seen him myself, I haven't, but I did see a stranger driving through the village a little while ago, so I did. Headed up towards Hideaway Hill, he was. I suppose it's quite romantic. Not sure how young Lucas will take it, mind.' Meg emptied the contents of her glass in three large gulps and passed it back towards Janet.

Janet had been wiping down the bar, but she stopped

at the mention of Lucas' name.

'Lucas? This is about Lucas?'

Meg Stanbridge shook her mop of grey curls. 'Lordy, Lordy me, no. Not exactly. About the lovely young Rachel, it is. Seems she has a boyfriend, it does. Leastways, that's what the stranger told Audrey Stelling he was. And Audrey Stelling told me. She overheard him asking the dear Reverend whether this was the road to the holiday cottages. Said his girlfriend was staying in one of them, he did. Well... There's only one girl that could possibly be, there is. And that's the lovely young Rachel, so it is. Another rum and black please, Janet, when you have the time.'

Janet reached for the glass and spotted Lucas standing just a few feet away to the left, with Ned and Gabriel. She stared at Lucas' face. It was the colour of the tea towel she was holding – off-white with just a hint of grey. She hadn't noticed him come in but from the look on his face, he had heard every word. And he didn't look happy. Not one little bit.

Chapter Twenty-Five

Rachel didn't know whether she was coming or going. Her head was in a whirl and her heart was in turmoil. Drew turning up on her doorstep had been a complete surprise. The last thing she expected and the last person she could have imagined opening the door to find standing before her. She almost wished she hadn't let him in. After the way he had treated her she would have been completely justified in slamming the door in his face.

But she hadn't. She had let him in. And he had told her that he wanted her back. That he still loved her. Although he hadn't actually said those words.

She had been wrong about him. He hadn't cheated. He hadn't lied. Jenny wasn't having his baby. He wasn't going to marry her. He didn't even love her. In fact, he was going to fire her. How could Rachel have got things so completely wrong?

It hadn't all been her fault though. Drew had said they should "take a break". He had ignored her phone calls and her texts and notes. He hadn't seemed to care that her heart was breaking. All he'd thought about was himself and what he wanted.

Apparently, he had finally made a decision. A

decision about their future. About Rachel's future. Although he hadn't consulted her. Not until now at least. And even now he wasn't discussing it. He wasn't asking Rachel's opinion. He didn't even ask the question. Not in so many words.

After he followed her into the kitchen and she had realised how wrong she had been, it took a while for her to calm down. To take in what he had said. Once she'd done that, Drew had asked again for a coffee and Rachel had made it.

Then Drew said: 'I needed time to think, Rach, and I have. We've been together for three years now and on the whole it's pretty good. My career's going well and your job's obviously secure. I think it's time we bought a place. A place of our own. I think we should move in together. I expect in time you'll want to do the whole marriage bit, although still not sure how I feel about that. I'll never cheat on you, even though you seem to think I could. And I'll never leave you like my dad left us. I'm just not sure we need a piece of paper. Maybe we do. Marriage has its benefits, I suppose. I need to think about that some more. We can get married if you want. It's probably not a bad idea. I've missed you, Rach. More than I thought I would.'

He moved towards her and took her in his arms. She couldn't speak. She couldn't think. She wasn't even sure what was happening. Until he kissed her.

'No.' Rachel pushed him away with both hands and he almost stumbled. 'No, Drew.'

He blinked several times. 'No? What d'you mean, no? No to what? To marriage? Well, I don't really care about the marriage bit. I thought that's what you would want.'

'No. Not to you anyway. No to marriage. No to living together. No to us dating. No to everything. No to you even being here. I meant what I said, Drew. I'm sorry that I thought you would cheat on me. I should've known you wouldn't. But you did treat me badly. Relationships are about discussing things together. We don't do that. We used to, I think. But now we don't. I don't want you back, Drew. It's over. I mean that. We're not on a break. We're broken up. And when you've finished your coffee, I want you to leave.'

His mouth fell open and he stared at her. 'You're dumping me?'

'Yes, Drew. I am. But I wish you all the best.'

Without another word, Drew turned and walked away.

Rachel expected to feel sad but she didn't. She felt happy. She felt optimistic. She felt... like dancing. Like dancing in the rain.

She ran into the hall and grabbed her coat.

Chapter Twenty-Six

'You're saturated!' Janet said, as Rachel strolled into The Snowdrop Inn, shortly after two-fifteen.

'It's raining,' Rachel replied, squeezing her way through to the bar.

Janet gave her an odd look. 'I know it's raining. But you look as if you've been swimming in the sea. Is it really that bad out there now?'

Rachel shook her head and grinned. 'I've been dancing.'

Janet's eyes narrowed. 'In the rain?'

Rachel nodded. 'Yep. It's packed in here. I can't see Lucas. Is he here?'

'Ah. About that. I hear you've had a visitor.'

'A visitor? Oh. You mean Drew.'

Janet tutted. '"Oh. You mean Drew,"' she repeated, in a coquettish voice. 'Yes, I mean Drew. What happened? Where is he? Are you back together? I know this is none of my business but I'm asking nevertheless.'

'He's gone home and no, we're not back together. We're finished for good.'

'Are you happy or sad about that? I assume, as you've been dancing in the rain, you're happy.'

Rachel laughed and nodded. 'Yes, I am. Oh, it turns

out that Jenny isn't expecting Drew's baby. She just wanted me to think that. It came as a complete shock when I told Drew about my conversation with her. He's furious. But more about the fact that she's got a crush on him and he'll have to get rid of her and find a new secretary than anything else.'

'Gosh. He did want you back then?'

'Apparently. He told me that he'd thought about it and decided we should live together. He even said we could get married if I want.'

'And they say romance is dead. But that's a biggie. You said no?'

Rachel nodded. 'Emphatically.'

'Good for you. What can I get you? It's on me.'

'Thanks but I'd rather find Lucas.'

'Oh yes. Lucas. Good luck with that. Meg Stanbridge brought us all some news, earlier and Lucas heard it. He knows that Drew was here and he didn't look pleased. The last time I saw him was about half an hour ago. He was staggering out of here with Gabriel. They said something about going for a curry and the nearest place to get one of those is Eastbourne. They may be gone for some time.'

'But... I thought we were going to spend the afternoon together. I thought... Where's Monty? Did he go with them?'

Janet tipped her head towards her private snug. 'He's in there with Merlot. I said I'd look after him. They're both curled up in front of the fire, and Mistletoe, my cat, is snuggled between them. You're welcome to go through.'

'That means he'll be coming back here to get Monty.'

'I suppose it does. But I wouldn't like to guess when. So, why don't you and I find a quiet corner and have that drink? My staff can cope fine without me.'

156

'That sounds like a very good idea. I think I need one.'

Chapter Twenty-Seven

'Hi,' Holly said, walking towards the table at which Rachel and Janet had been sitting for about half an hour. She dropped down into the chair beside her mum and kissed her on the cheek. 'Gabriel just called. He asked if I'd come and get Monty because Lucas' ankle is bad again. They're getting a cab from Eastbourne and going directly back to the cottages.'

'I'm surprised he can feel it,' Janet said. 'He had quite a lot to drink earlier and I expect they've had a few beers with their curry.'

Holly rolled her eyes. 'Gabriel was slurring. So enough said really. They'll both be fine if they sleep it off for an hour or two this afternoon.' She glanced at Rachel. 'Gabriel told me that your ex is here. Is that true?'

Rachel nodded. 'He was. He's not here now.'

'Sent him packing, did you?'

'Let's just say, I've realised there are plenty more fish in the sea, as my mum always says.' She grinned at Holly.

'And one of those fish is called Lucas.'

'Who is more than happy to be caught,' Janet said,

'unless I'm very much mistaken.'

'He must like me, mustn't he?' Rachel asked. 'To react the way you said he did.'

'What?' Holly queried, with a grin. 'Get drunk and go for a curry. Definitely. On top of which, Gabriel said that he thinks Lucas has "got it bad" because all he could talk about was how wonderful this week had been until today. It's done nothing but bloody rain since you two got here, so he clearly wasn't talking about the weather. The guy's 'in lurve', Rachel.'

Rachel's cheeks burned. 'I don't know about that. I do think he likes me, but his girlfriend dumped him recently, and I've just come out of a relationship. I don't think he wants to rush into anything. Neither of us do. We're just friends.'

'Yeah yeah. Blah blah. Friends indeed. You want to be more than friends, admit it. And so does he.'

'Okay, I admit it. I'm not sure how Lucas feels though.'

'Especially as he thinks you're probably back with your ex,' Janet said. 'The sooner you put him straight on that score the better.' She got to her feet. 'I'll get Monty then Holly can give you a lift back. You *danced* here, didn't you?' She winked and walked away.'

'Danced?' Holly queried.

'In the rain.' Rachel laughed. 'I was happy.'

'You're insane. Come on then. Let's get you home you Darcey Bussell wannabe.'

Chapter Twenty-Eight

Rachel hurried along the hall of Mistletoe Cottage towards the front door, not knowing what to think. She didn't know what she had expected Lucas to do when she and Holly returned with Monty, but she hadn't expected him to be sound asleep on the sofa. The door was unlocked so she'd let herself in and no matter how much noise she made, Lucas would not wake up.

For once, Monty flatly refused to bark, or make any noise at all. It was as if he knew his master needed sleep and was determined not to be the one to wake him. He curled up on the rug in front of the unlit wood burner and went to sleep. Rachel had to move him to light it, but even then he didn't make a sound. She was about to give up hope and go back to her own cottage when she suddenly heard Lucas' voice.

'Rachel? What are you doing here?'

'Bringing your dog back, and lighting your fire.'

Lucas glanced at Monty and the blazing logs in the wood burner and rubbed his eyes.

'How long have I been asleep?'

'For several hours. It's getting on for six.'

'Christ. Why didn't you wake me?'

'Believe me, Lucas, I tried.'

160

'Oh. I've been told that it's like trying to wake the dead after I've had couple of drinks.'

'A couple of barrels from what I hear. Not that that matters. And who told you that? Your ex?' Why was she feeling jealous about that? Holly was right. She was insane.

'Lucas gave her an odd look. 'My mates.'

'Oh.'

'Talking of exes. Where's yours? Is he still an ex? Or are you back together?'

'No. He's an ex. A permanent ex.'

Lucas brightened at that. 'Your choice?'

Rachel nodded. 'My choice.'

'Excellent decision.'

'What about you?'

He blinked repeatedly. 'Me?'

'If your ex turned up and asked you to go back with her, would you?'

He looked relieved, as if that wasn't the question he had expected her to ask.

'No way. We were together for a year and now that I look back on it, that was probably ten months too long. We had nothing in common. We didn't even like the same things. Apart from sex. Sorry. No idea why I said that.'

The room seemed hotter suddenly and Rachel moved further away from the wood burner.

'I only went out with her in the first place,' he continued, 'because one of my mates was dating her best friend who for some strange reason, thought we would be good together. We weren't. Not really. Oh. Was that thunder rumbling in the distance?'

'No.' Rachel blushed. 'It was my stomach. I haven't eaten anything all day. Holly and I stopped on the way back, and I bought a fabulous-looking coffee and walnut cake from Maisy Miller's bakery. I was just going to have some.'

'I've got a better idea. Why don't I cook you dinner?'

'Oh. Are you up to that?'

'I can cook.' He sounded a little offended.

'I thought you said you couldn't.'

He grinned. 'I can throw together one or two things. Don't worry, I won't poison you.'

'But you had curry for lunch. Are you hungry?'

His eyes flashed and he coughed lightly. 'I could eat.'

'Then I'd love that. May I go and take a shower and get changed first? I got soaked earlier and I'm covered in mud.'

'Of course you can. Are you going to wear that pretty dress? Because I'm telling you now, I won't be able to keep my eyes off you if you do.'

'Oh wow.' She quickly turned and headed towards the door. 'I won't wear that one again but I do have another which is equally… pretty.'

'Hurry back,' he called after her. 'I'll open a bottle of wine.'

She opened the front door and a gust of icy wind hit her full on, making her stumble backwards. The row of pictures hanging on the wall in the hallway rattled like a set of chattering teeth and the jackets on the coat hooks flapped like trapped birds.

'Bloody hell!' she yelled, pushing the door closed with some effort and heading back to the sitting room. 'It's *really* cold and windy out there. In fact, it's blowing a gale. I wouldn't be surprised if there was a hurricane on the way.'

'We'd better batten down the hatches then,' Lucas said, grinning.

'I'm serious, Lucas. It's really getting bad. I'm thinking more along the lines of, perhaps we'd better

162

evacuate. These cottages are so exposed and the cliff's already eroded by another few feet this week, according to Jarvis Pope. He was in The Snowdrop Inn this afternoon when I was waiting for you. I jokingly told Sonia the other day that I wouldn't be surprised to wake up on the beach one of these mornings. It doesn't seem so amusing when there's a chance I might.'

Lucas picked up his phoned and swiped the screen. 'According to the Met Office there'll be gale force winds and driving rain. There are several flood warnings in place, although I can't see any for around here, so I think we're safe on that score.' He looked up at Rachel and smiled. 'These cottages have been here since the mid-1800s and this definitely won't be the first storm they've withstood. Now if we were in a caravan, or worse still, a tent, then I *would* be worried. But I think we'll be fine if we just shut the doors and windows and stay inside.'

'And what if Monty wants to pee?'

'Ah. Well… he's pretty good at holding it but if the worst comes to the worst then, as unhygienic as it may be, there's always the bucket and several sheets of newspaper.'

'For a moment I thought you were going to suggest the shower.'

Lucas grinned. 'Well…' He laughed and shook his head. 'I don't think it'll come to that. Let's see what happens. In the meantime, why don't we have a cup of tea and a slice of that delicious-sounding cake you got from… where did you say? Oh I remember… Maisy Miller's bakery and I'll start making dinner. It might be one of those storms that's over very quickly and isn't anywhere near as bad as you think.'

'Or it might be like that Great Storm all those years ago. I'll put the kettle on but if I hear so much as one piece of rock tumble from this cliff, or one roof tile rattle, we're getting out of here and heading for The Snowdrop Inn, no matter what. Actually, perhaps that's what we should do anyway – before the weather gets too bad for us to go anywhere. At least there'll be others in the pub.'

'And alcohol is better than tea in a crisis, is that what you're saying?'

'No. But the pub's relatively sheltered by the other side of this cliff and the rest of the village, so...'

Lucas grinned as Rachel's voice trailed off.

'So... let's go to The Snowdrop Inn,' he said. 'But you'll have to do the driving. Apart from my ankle playing up again this afternoon, I had far, far too much to drink at lunchtime.' He got to his feet with some effort. 'Was that the doorbell?'

Rachel glanced towards the hall. 'I think it was.' She headed towards the door but this time, she held the door with both hands as she opened it and sheltered behind it as much as she could.

'Are you and Lucas okay?' Gabriel yelled, above the whoosh and hiss of the wind. He looked concerned. 'This is going to be a pretty bad storm, I think.'

Rachel nodded vigorously. 'You're not kidding. We've decided to go to the pub to ride it out.'

Gabriel shook his head. 'Not possible, I'm afraid. Henry's just called to warn us that a sinkhole's appeared in the middle of Hideaway Hill. It's about three feet deep and the same wide, if not more. Because the road's so narrow, no car will be able to get past it. He's roping off the road so that no one unwittingly drives into the thing.'

'A sinkhole?' Lucas said, from the doorway of the sitting room. 'That's incredible. Come in out of the wind, Gabriel.'

'Oh yes, sorry,' Rachel added. 'Come in.'

Gabriel shook his head. 'Thanks, but I just wanted to check on you and tell you about the hole. Jarvis told

Henry that he thinks it may be due to one of the tributaries from Hideaway Hole. They're probably all swollen because of the amount of rain we've had this week and water will find any weak spots underground and wash away loose rock and earth. Don't look so worried, Rachel. We're far enough away and it won't affect these cottages. We're safe up here, trust me.'

Rachel wasn't convinced, but she was certain that if Gabriel, or Holly, or Janet, or any of the villagers come to that, thought there was any real danger to Gilroy's Happy Holiday Cottages and the occupants, they would say so. That eased her anxiety a little.

'We could get to the village across the fields,' Gabriel was saying, 'but I honestly think we'd all simply be better off just staying indoors. Henry told me that even his tractor is struggling in the mud, and this awful wind and rain is simply making conditions worse. Do you need anything? You've got the lanterns if there's another power cut but you're more than welcome to come and join me and Holly in Holly Cottage, if you like. We'd be happy to have you.'

'Thanks,' Lucas said. 'But I think it's best if I stay here. Monty hates storms and his barking may drive you nuts. I'm used to it so it doesn't bother me.'

'We wouldn't mind, but it's up to you. What about you, Rachel?' Gabriel asked. 'You don't want to be alone, do you? Or are you going to stay here with Lucas?'

'Um.' Rachel glanced from Gabriel to Lucas.

'You're more than welcome to keep me and Monty company,' Lucas said. 'But if you'd—'

'Great,' she said before he had a chance to tell her she could go to Holly and Gabriel's. 'I'll stay with you and Monty. Besides, you need someone to make your tea and run around after you, especially since you consumed so

165

much alcohol at lunchtime.'

'That's true,' Lucas said, and there was something in his eyes that sent sparks shooting through her.

'Okay then. We'll be here if you need us,' Gabriel said. 'Just call. You've got Holly's number on the key tags, remember. See you all when it's over.' He grinned, then turned and ran down the path.

Rachel shoved the door closed and turned to face Lucas. A wave of warmth immediately washed over her. It may have been because she had finally shut out the awful weather, or it may have been because of the way he was looking at her. He was standing in the middle of the hallway and she would have to squeeze past him unless he moved, and he didn't seem to have any immediate intention of doing that.

'Well then,' she said, leaning back against the door. 'It looks as if we're stuck here. Any suggestions as to how we should pass the time?'

A smouldering hot smile crept across his face. 'One or two things spring to mind,' he said, 'but I'm not sure whether you'd be interested.'

She studied his face for a moment. The curve of his lips; the twinkle in his eyes; the slight tilt of his head and the firmness of his clean-shaven jaw. She was often mistaken about what men were thinking, or intending, or saying, but she didn't think she was mistaken about what was on Lucas' mind. And when he held his hand out towards her, she knew she understood exactly what he meant.

'Oh, I'm interested, Lucas,' she said, easing herself away from the door and slipping her hand into his. 'Very, very interested.'

He closed his fingers around hers and pulled her into his arms.

'You have no idea how pleased I am to hear you say

166

that,' he said.

Then he kissed her so deeply and passionately that she almost completely forgot about the storm.

Until Monty came careering down the hall and tried to squeeze himself between them.

Lucas smiled at her like a man who had touched the moon, and was hoping to do so again.

'We have two options,' he said, his voice husky with desire. 'Either the sitting room, where Monty will no doubt climb all over us, or...' His glance drifted towards the stairs.

Rachel smiled. 'The 'or' option, I think.'

Lucas beamed. 'He'll probably still climb all over us, but if we give him five minutes, he'll eventually settle at the foot of the bed, or if we're very lucky, in his own bed.'

'I can spare five minutes,' Rachel said, tracing a line around Lucas' neck with one finger. 'But only because I love Monty almost as much as I do you. Oh! But not in the same way, of course. And I didn't mean I love you. I mean, I really, really like you and...' She felt the blood rush to her cheeks. 'I mean I... um.'

Lucas smiled and kissed her again, even though Monty was sitting on both Lucas' feet and hers.

'Don't worry, Rachel,' Lucas said, when he finally released her. 'I know exactly what you mean. And I really, *really*, like you too.'

Then he turned towards the stairs with one arm still wrapped tightly around her and they walked along the hall with Monty following right at their heels... and Lucas hardly limping at all.

Chapter Twenty-Nine

Rachel and Lucas lay wrapped in each other's arms some considerable time later, with Monty squashed between them, his nose nuzzled against Lucas' neck and his front paws resting in one of Rachel's hands. The bedroom curtains were closed to shut out the dreadful weather but when Rachel briefly went downstairs to get them both some water, the storm was in full force. The wind banged on the doors, rattled the windows and whistled down the chimney. It battered the garden fences and, as she watched from the kitchen, it tore up the panels as if they were made of paper. Several midnight-blue painted slats flew through the air like spears, probably never to be seen again.

As she hurried back upstairs to share the news with Lucas, it sounded as if Thor himself was on the roof, bashing the tiles with his hammer and she was sure she heard a row of slate tiles ripped loose from their nails, in what probably would have looked like a *Mexican wave* to anyone foolish enough to be standing outside to see it.

'Yes,' Lucas said, when she handed him his water and told him what she'd seen and heard. 'It sounded as if the roof was coming off but I'm sure it's not as bad as that. Vine Cottage, being the end-of-terrace facing the path of the storm, will probably bear the brunt of the damage. Although all four cottages are no doubt taking a beating. As Gabriel mentioned earlier though, this isn't the first storm these cottages have seen, and it won't be the last.'

'We hope,' Rachel said, moving Monty over slightly so that she could get back into bed and snuggle up against Lucas. She was glad she didn't have to go through this alone. She was trying to tell herself that it was just a storm, especially as Lucas didn't seem unduly worried, but she'd never heard a building creak and groan as much as this, and she had visions of all four cottages flying through the air, like Dorothy's home had done in *The Wizard of Oz*.

'Don't worry, Rachel,' Lucas said, reassuringly, as if reading her mind. 'The cottages may be battered and bruised but they'll stand their ground and show what they are made of.'

'Hmm... in more ways than one, I expect. The roof timbers are probably exposed and we'll probably wake up, rain drenched and staring at the sky. Not that I'll be able to get any sleep at all with this going on.'

Lucas smiled and kissed her. 'You're right about not getting any sleep, gorgeous, but it'll have more to do with me not being able to keep my hands off you than it will some noisy old storm.'

Just to prove his point, he pulled her closer and kissed her again, and Monty moved down the bed to get out of their way, as if he knew they wanted some space.

Chapter Thirty

The storm lasted for most of the night and it left a trail of debris and detritus in its wake. Holly Cottage, together with Ivy Cottage held up well with only a few tiles missing from the roofs and all the garden fences gone. Mistletoe Cottage suffered only loose roof tiles but several garden fence panels had disappeared completely.

Vine Cottage came off worst. It was the first of the cottages in the path of the storm and subsequently bore the full force of the impact. The chimney stack collapsed inwards, smashing through the roof, the main bedroom and the sitting room taking several more bricks with it on its way down. If Billy Brookes had been in his bed, he would probably be dead this morning.

Luckily for him – in more ways than one – he wasn't in his bed. He was in Janet Gilroy's. Because Janet had made a decision. A decision about her love life. It was time she put the past behind her and threw caution to the wind. She liked Billy and he liked her and she didn't care what anyone thought. Her daughters loved her and so did Gramps, and she knew that as long as she was happy, they wouldn't object to anything she did.

She was well aware that Ivy and Holly felt she could do better than Billy but again she didn't care. In just a

few days she had come to know the real Billy Brookes –
the man who kept his 'real self' hidden from the world.
He was kind, sensitive, thoughtful and loving. On top of
all that, he was pretty good in bed, as she had discovered
last night.

He had even set her mind at rest about the storm and
Skylar Lake's prediction.

When she'd shared her concerns with Kev-the-Rev
earlier in the week, she'd been surprised by his response.
All the usually sensible Kevin Longbourne would say
was that fortune telling was very hit and miss and
shouldn't be taken as gospel. Whereas, the gospel
should. Despite the fact she didn't believe in God, he had
told her to trust in the Lord. In her opinion, that was
about as much use as a wine barrel full of holes. But he
had told her one thing she knew made sense. That
worrying about it wouldn't change anything and that if
she really believed someone's life depended on her
making the right decision, she needed to think very
carefully about any decisions she made.

On the day of the storm, she had been panicking all
afternoon as the wind increased intensity. Billy had
asked why she was so concerned and she told him the
whole story. Well, most of it. She left out the bits about
the 'B'.

Billy's answer was simple: 'People die all the time,'
he said. 'And for every death there's always someone
who feels they could have said something, or done
something, or somehow made a difference. But the plain
fact is, in the majority of cases, they probably couldn't.
This, Skylar Lake woman said it will depend on your
decision. So don't make any decisions. Or if you really
have to, then come and ask me. Together, I'm one
hundred per cent certain we'll make the right decision.
But if there is the tiniest chance we got it wrong, I'll

171

share the responsibility. I'll share the burden.'

It sounded ridiculous. It was almost like passing the buck. And yet it comforted her on so many levels. It made her feel at ease. That was the moment she decided that Billy Brookes would be spending the night with her. And she told him so. Straightaway.

Chapter Thirty-One

Billy Brookes scratched his head and rubbed his chin. He then scribbled something down in the notepad he carried. He'd been wandering around the cottages for almost an hour now doing exactly the same thing. Every time he came into view in front of her kitchen window, Holly watched him closely.

She still couldn't believe that her mum had asked Billy to carry out the repairs to all four cottages before she'd even seen an estimate, but all Janet would say on the subject was that builders were like gold dust. She reminded Holly how difficult it had been to find a builder to do the refurbishment at The Snowdrop Inn, and that, until Billy had shown up, Janet had been looking for over six months without success.

'Billy's only been here for a couple of days,' Janet said, 'and not only did he start work the minute he said he would, unlike the previous ones who didn't even bother to turn up, he's already transformed one of those odd-shaped rooms in the roof. Just imagine how much will get done once his team of builders arrive.'

That was a prospect Holly was not looking forward to; for some reason she couldn't quite put her finger on it. And the fact that Janet also thought Billy had 'long-term boyfriend potential' proved to Holly just how desperate things had become, not simply regarding the refurbishment work Janet wanted done at the pub, but also with Janet's love life. As far as Holly was concerned, believing that Billy Brookes had any 'boyfriend potential' at all, let alone long-term was akin to suggesting that the ancient rust bucket of a black sports car he drove was really a Jaguar F-TYPE.

Even if Holly could overlook the fact that the man strutted around like a peacock, had wild looking hair and enough stubble on his chin to make a hedgehog proud, she couldn't ignore his fondness for the use of the word, 'love'. When she'd spoken to him earlier, to see if he could give her a rough idea of the likely cost, he must've used the word at least ten times.

'Those fence panels don't come cheap, love,' he'd said, and: 'The roof repairs alone are going to cost a tidy little packet, love', and: 'We'll need a scaffold, love, which would cost an arm and a leg at the best of times but when you want one in a hurry, well, I have to tell you, love, you're talking along the lines of an arm, a leg and several other body parts.'

She was almost fit to scream: 'Stop bloody calling me 'love'!' but fortunately for everyone, Gabriel had come outside, taken her by the arm and said that she was needed on the phone – even though that wasn't actually true. He merely used it to 'get her away' before she said something he thought she would later regret.

'Don't you worry about a thing, love,' Billy called after her as she and Gabriel were walking back to Holly Cottage. 'Everything will be fine, love. You can count on me.'

'Leave it,' Gabriel said, obviously reading her mind. 'Your mum thinks he's the answer to all her prayers, and perhaps he is. There's no point in causing a row just because he repeatedly uses a particular word which you happen to find irritating. And you may not have noticed, but he only seems to use it when he's in 'builder mode'.'

'What?' Holly hadn't noticed.

Gabriel nodded and smiled. 'It's true. He hasn't said it once when we've seen him in the pub, or out and about, and when I asked Janet if he dropped it into their conversations, she gave me a very odd look and asked why on earth Billy would call her 'love'.'

'How bizarre.' Holly glanced back at Billy as he scratched his head, rubbed his chin and scribbled something else down in his notepad.

'I think it's like an office worker wearing a suit,' Gabriel said. 'Billy puts on his 'builder persona' and suddenly every few words coming out of his mouth have the word 'love' attached.'

'Well, that's rather odd. I'm not sure mum should be dating a man who changes the way he speaks depending on what he's doing at the time.'

'I don't think it's a problem, darling. Not really. And the guy seems like a genuinely decent man. I believe he's as honest and trustworthy as anyone else we know and he definitely seems exceptionally keen on Janet – which I suspect, if you're being honest with yourself, is the real issue here. You want your mum to be happy and you want her to find love again, but you want it to be with a man whom you think is suitable, and unfortunately that's not the way it works... love.' Gabriel nudged Holly's arm and winked at her.

'Don't you start,' Holly said, with a smile. She glanced back at Billy one final time before going inside Holly Cottage. 'Perhaps you're right. Perhaps I need to give the guy a chance. But he's certainly not what Ivy and I had pictured as a potential step-father.'

'Please don't tell him that,' Gabriel said, as he closed

the door behind them. 'And definitely don't tell Janet.'

Holly watched Billy more intently now, as she filled the kettle to make coffee for herself and Gabriel. The man did have a disarming smile. And a cheeky wink. And judging by the number of times he seemed to be writing in his notebook, the price he was probably intending to charge for the repairs would be enough for him to be able to afford a Jaguar F-TYPE. A brand new one, more than likely. She just hoped her mum wouldn't get a very nasty and unwelcome surprise.

But Gabriel was probably right. Would she and Ivy ever really feel that any man would be good enough for their mum? She needed to give him a chance, if only for her mum's sake. And perhaps a quiet word in his ear would do the trick. She could simply tell him that she hated being called, 'love', and ask if he would stop.

She opened the kitchen window a fraction.

'I'm making coffee, Billy. Would you like one?'

The cheeky smile appeared. 'Thanks. I'd kill for a cup. Lots of milk and two sugars please, love.'

Holly closed her eyes and gritted her teeth. The sooner she had a word with him, the happier she would be.

Chapter Thirty-Two

Rachel and Lucas stood arm in arm looking up at the cottages. Monty was collecting twigs and broken branches and dropping them at their feet. Rachel smiled down at him and then up into Lucas' eyes.

'It's going to take a long time for Hideaway Down to get back to normal, isn't it?'

Lucas nodded. 'There was quite a lot of minor damage to several properties in the village, according to Billy. He also said that Meg Stanbridge came charging into the pub this morning, yelling at the top of her voice that Janet and Billy had saved the lives of her geese.'

'The Gaggle Gang?'

Lucas laughed. 'Yep. I shouldn't laugh. It would've been awful if those geese had died. They live in some sort of shed in her garden, apparently. She was moaning in the pub about how much rain had come in during that storm last Friday night, so Janet asked Billy if he could patch it up a bit. He started it yesterday morning before the storm hit but he told Meg that she'd have to keep the geese somewhere else because he'd need to take part of the shed down and rebuild it. Janet asked Kev-the-Rev if the geese could stay in an outhouse attached to the church hall and he agreed, so that's where they were last night. Along with Meg herself. The storm completely destroyed her old shed and took several tiles off the roof of her house which came crashing down on top of the shed. So if the geese had been there…'

'Oh my God. That's unbelievable.'

'The universe works in mysterious ways.'

Rachel smiled. 'While you were talking to Billy, Holly told me that because of the sinkhole, no cars can get up or down Hideaway Hill. The only way to and from the village is on foot or Henry's tractor.'

'That means we'll be walking to the pub, I guess.'

'It means more than that. It means we won't be able to get our cars out tomorrow.'

Lucas frowned. 'That hadn't even occurred to me.'

'Holly also said that due to the damage to the cottages, Janet has cancelled the reservations for the people coming to stay from Friday night onwards. Your cottage will be fine because there's only a few loose tiles and Billy told Holly that he could get those done today. He could probably fix the tiles on my cottage too, he told her. But Janet feels that with the work going on, on Vine Cottage, it wouldn't be right to have paying guests in Mistletoe and Ivy Cottages.'

Lucas looked concerned. 'Does she want us to leave?'

Rachel turned to face him. 'No. She told Holly to speak to us and see what we wanted to do, but as we can't get our cars out, if we want to stay for the weekend, we can stay for free. And if we want to stay on for a few more days, she's happy for us to do that too, providing Billy says it's safe for all of us to be here. Of course she won't tell the insurance company that, or anyone else. It'll just be our little secret.'

Lucas laughed. 'And everyone else's in Hideaway Down.' He looked into her eyes. 'Do you want to stay?'

She looked back into his. 'I do. I spoke to Mum, and she said that she can cope perfectly well without me for a few more days, providing I'm safe and happy. And I am.'

'I don't have to be back at work until Monday, and even then, if I tell my partners I want to stay on here, they won't object. In fact, they'll be happy for me.'

'Shall we stay then? Providing Billy says it's safe to do so?'

Lucas pulled her close. 'Yes. But if Billy says it's not, there's bound to be a hotel in Eastbourne that accepts dogs.'

Rachel smiled up at him. 'There are a few missing tiles on my roof, whereas none are missing on yours. Perhaps...'

'We should both stay in Mistletoe Cottage. Is that what you mean?'

'Only if you think that's a good idea.'

He held her tighter to him. 'I think that's a very good idea, Rachel. In fact I think that's absolutely brilliant.'

Monty gave three loud barks and Lucas laughed.

'That meant: 'I agree, Lucas.''

Rachel laughed too. 'Did it? I thought it meant: 'Kiss Rachel now.''

'Hmm. We're clearly having some language problems. But I think I prefer your translation.'

'So do I, Lucas.'

Monty barked once.

'So does he,' Lucas said, grinning.

Then he kissed her as if he would never let her go, and Rachel knew she would come back to Hideaway Down in the future. But next time, she wouldn't be coming alone.

THE END

179

Thank you for reading, *Dancing in the Rain.* I hope you enjoyed it and if so, I would absolutely love it if you would consider telling your friends and/or posting a short review on Amazon. Word of mouth is an author's best friend and very much appreciated. Thanks so much.

Please take a look at the following page, for details of my next book: Deck the Halls.

COMING SOON

Deck the Halls

Will Harriet's Christmas sparkle?

Harriet Hall wants Christmas to be perfect in her ancestral home, The Hall, with roaring log fires, scented pine trees, sparkling decorations, and mouth-watering, festive feasts. The Hall may look like a dilapidated pile, but as she tells her family: 'It won't take long to spruce it up.'

Harriet's finally going to introduce the eccentric, Hall family, and The Hall to her boyfriend, Art (Arthur) and his parents, the Camlan-Browns. She wants to make a good impression because Art is the man she hopes to marry, even if he hasn't asked her yet.

Although agreeing to let Lance Knightly – her step-brother's drinking pal – do the renovation, may prove a big mistake. The man has an ego the size of The Hall and thinks it's fine to disagree with her – when he's not too busy flirting with every woman in sight... including her elderly aunt.

But when a heavy snowfall brings Harriet's plans – along with the stucco ceilings – crashing down around her, will it be Art who saves Harriet's Christmas, or will Lance turn into a knight in shining armour? Not that Harriet needs rescuing. She's perfectly capable of dealing with a crisis without the help of a man.

To see details of my other books, please go to the books page on my website or scan the QR code, below. www.emilyharvale.com/books.

***

Scan the code above to see Emily's books on Amazon

To read about me, my books, my work in progress and competitions, freebies, or to contact me, pop over to my website www.emilyharvale.com. To be the first to hear about new releases and other news, you can subscribe to my Readers' Club newsletter via the 'Sign me up' box. Or why not come and say 'Hello' on Facebook, Twitter, Instagram or Pinterest. Hope to chat with you soon.

18080269R00114

Printed in Great Britain
by Amazon